SLOW RIDE

a Playing for Keeps novella

CATHRYN FOX

D1714547

Previously released on Entangled's Flaunt imprint as *Cowboy's Way* – November 2013 and has been enhanced with new material.

Entangled Publishing, LLC
2614 South Timberline Road
Suite 109
Fort Collins, CO 80525
Visit our website at www.entangledpublishing.com.

Brazen is an imprint of Entangled Publishing, LLC. For more information on our titles, visit www.brazenbooks.com.

Edited by Candace Havens
Cover design by Heather Howland
Cover art from Shutterstock

Manufactured in the United States of America

First Edition September 2015

ENTANGLED
BRAZEN

This one is for Jan. You are the wind in my sails.

Chapter One

Ten years ago

Chase Cooper grabbed the strap on Jag's backpack and gave a good hard tug, hauling him back to the sidewalk seconds before an SUV would have slammed into him harder than their rival school's linebacker at the last football game. The driver blared his horn as he sped by, offering Coop and his two buddies his middle finger.

"Fuck you," Mac said, retaliating with two fingers as he shuffled on the curb, daring the guy to come back and fight.

"Huh?" Jag said, lifting his eyes from his phone.

Coop shook his head. "Are you trying to get yourself killed?" He looked over Jag's shoulder, trying to get a glimpse of his phone. "What are you watching that's so important, anyway?"

Mac jumped from the curb. "Probably porn," he supplied.

Jag grinned. "Fuck you." He powered his phone down

and shoved it into his low-hanging jeans.

"What the fuck is the matter with you, dude?" Coop checked traffic and darted across the street, the six beers he'd taken from his father's fridge banging together in his backpack.

"I need to get laid," Jag shot back. "That's what's the matter with me." Grinning, Jag shoved Coop toward a streetlight. "I don't get it on a daily basis like you do, asshole."

Coop moved around a lamppost and cut between houses, slipping through their yards to take a shortcut to Mari's house. "I told you, Mari and I are friends."

Mac snorted. "You mean fuck friends, right?"

Coop frowned and drove his hands in his pockets. "For the hundredth time, no, we don't fuck." Why was he even bothering to defend himself with these two wiseasses? "Just because we hang out, laugh, and have a great time together doesn't mean we're having sex."

Jag scoffed. "Then why is she always getting half naked in front of you?"

"She's a model." He pushed through her front gate. "She's used to wearing next to nothing."

Jag rubbed his hands together. "Just the way I like them."

They walked the pathway leading to Mari's front door, and Coop jumped onto the grass. "Come on," he said quietly.

Mac groaned. "Fuck's sake, Coop, why do we always have to go through the window? You got something against using the front door?" Keeping tight on his heels, his friends followed him around a bush to Mari's window.

The three of them had quite the reputation around town, and Mari's folks weren't all that fond of their daughter hanging out with them, which was why Coop went to great lengths to avoid a run-in with them. "I just prefer to use her window."

Jag bent and peered through the glass. "Is this the one you crawl in when she gets half naked for you?"

"Fuck off," Coop said, and quietly slid the glass up. The guys were wrong. He and Mari weren't having sex and never had. She might walk around half naked, and of course she was totally fuckable, but there was another girl he couldn't get out of his head—one who was off-limits and couldn't be bothered to give him the time of day anyway.

He threw his right leg over the windowsill and followed through with his hips, grunting at the tight squeeze.

"You might want to lay off those cheeseburgers, dude," Jag said.

Mac burst out laughing.

Closing his eyes, Coop prayed Mari's parents were heavy sleepers, because his ass hanging over the sill would make the perfect target for a load of buckshot. He pushed through, jumped to his feet, and waved the guys in.

Jag and Mac scrambled in behind him, giggling like little girls as they shoved at each other, then plunked themselves down on Mari's unmade bed. Coop glanced around, but Mari was nowhere to be found. A noise sounded from inside her big walk-in closet, and he motioned for the guys to be quiet.

Lowering his backpack to the floor, he crept across the carpet. Last week she'd sneaked up on him at the soccer field—damn near scared the shit out of him. She had a good laugh over that, but now tonight was payback.

He grabbed the double doors and flung them open. "Got ya…" His voice fell off when his eyes connected with Mari's twin sister—Mari's very *naked* twin sister.

Oh, shit.

As the girl of his dreams went poker straight before him, the dress in her hands fell from her fingers, making a *whoosh*ing sound as it sailed to the floor.

"I…uh…" His voice must have snapped her back.

"What the hell!" She quickly put her hands over her body and turned sideways, curving her back and giving him the sweetest, sexiest view of her perfect ass. Fuck.

Julia.

She might be Mari's twin, and he'd seen Mari's body numerous times, but it didn't compare to Julia's. His cock thickened, and at the base of his neck, his pulse jackhammered. Christ, he wanted her in the worst way, but she was his best friend's sister and he had been warned that she was off-limits.

"Get out," she said, a pink flush moving up her neck to her cheeks. "I'm not Mari."

His friends laughed, and Coop clenched his teeth, ready to kill them. But if he moved, he'd expose her, and he wasn't about to cause her any more embarrassment. He glanced over his shoulder. "Cut it out," he warned and widened his stance to block their view and give her the privacy she deserved.

"Now," she said.

He grabbed a fistful of hair. "Look, I'm…I'm…a…"

She leveled him with a stare, those whiskey eyes with the honey flecks holding him in place. "Is 'pervert' the word you're looking for?" she asked.

He wanted to leave, to drag his eyes from her, but honor was waging war with his dick…and losing. Plus he'd flung the doors open, and if he backed up now, his friends would see her. He grabbed Mari's robe hanging on the inside hook bedside him, handed it to her, and forced his eyes to the shoe box over her head as she snatched it from him.

"Listen, I'm sorry. I thought you were…"

"I know who you thought I was."

Cotton rasped over her skin, and he envied the robe as she pulled it on. "If I'd have known it was you in here, I would have just left"—he paused and jerked his thumb over his shoulder—"and dragged those two assholes with me. I'd never want to walk in on you naked, Julia. Never. It was a mistake."

"I know," she said, her voice going so low, he had to strain to hear it. "I'm not my sister."

His gaze darted back to hers, and his throat tightened when he saw the pained look on her face. What the hell? Did she think she wasn't as beautiful as Mari, as desirable? That he would have just left, because *her* nakedness was repulsive or something? She might not be as outgoing or popular as her sister, but that didn't mean he didn't want her—or didn't want to see her naked. Because hell yeah, he did. Right now just wasn't the right time, and he was trying his damnedest to be respectful, no matter how thick his dick was or how badly it was begging him for a little action.

"Julia," he said, touching a strand of her long dark hair. "I didn't mean—"

"What's happening here?" Mari said from her doorway. Coop spun around and found Mari staring at him, dressed in a barely-there bikini, her hands on her hips. She cocked her head. "Is there something I should know?"

"I thought she was you," Coop explained.

Julia pushed past him, "I was looking for that dress I lent you when your boyfriend found me. He didn't know it was me until I told him."

Mari rolled her eyes. "You'd think you could tell us apart by now."

He could. They were identical, but to him they were night and day. "Wait, I can tell—"

"And you never have to worry about anything happening." Julia turned and met his glance straight on. "He's not my type."

Mari zeroed in on his backpack on the floor and bounded toward it. "Did you bring the beer for the beach party?"

No longer in the mood to party, he watched Julia disappear. Christ, he might have just saved Jag from getting run over, but he was the one feeling like he'd just been steamrolled.

Chapter Two

Julia Blair didn't like surprises, and she liked cryptic messages delivered after midnight even less. She shut the door behind the stranger.

The old wooden floors creaked as she made her way back down the hall of her condo and into her living room. Fighting off a shiver, she tugged her cotton robe tighter around her waist and pushed aside the case files she'd been going over. She sat down in her comfy recliner, read "Ms. Blair" on the envelope, and then turned it over in her hand. She honestly had no idea who'd be delivering a letter to her so late at night, but couldn't discount the possibility that it had come from McGinley and Gregors, the law firm where she worked.

In the window behind her sofa, the air conditioner clanked and coughed like an asthma patient, and she nearly jumped out of her recliner. Living alone smack-dab in the middle of downtown Halifax, she always exercised caution, and at first she wasn't even going to open the door. But when she peeked through her curtains and spotted the courier van, she went ahead and answered, figuring it might be the files she'd been expecting.

Inside, she found what appeared to be an invitation from the owner of a dude ranch. Crinkling her nose in surprise, she read the script. This had to be a mistake. Who would be inviting her to a one-week, all-inclusive vacation to a dude ranch in Alberta beginning this Saturday night, a mere two days away? She sank deeper into her chair, put her feet up, and searched her memory bank. She didn't know anyone in Alberta, let alone anyone who owned a dude ranch. Could it have been an old client?

She grabbed her tablet, punched in the information, and discovered that the ranch and airline voucher were indeed legit. Intriguing. She dug deeper around the ranch's website, hoping to figure out who owned it, but her search came up empty. She peered into the envelope and pulled out a slip of paper. On it she read, "A week of fun and relaxation from your high school secret admirer."

High school secret admirer?

She went on to read the cryptic words, "I'll even watch *High in the Sky* with you," and stiffened. Since *High in the Sky* was her favorite movie, whoever sent this invitation knew her very well.

But who?

She thought about the crowd she'd hung with years ago. They all knew she'd loved that particular movie, but she couldn't imagine any one of the guys from her clique having a secret crush on her or sending her such a mysterious invitation. The invite had to be for her impetuous sister, Mari, who shared the same tastes as Julia. As a swimsuit model, picking up and flying off to exotic locales was something her sister did on a regular basis. She wasn't in one place long enough to bother with an apartment, and just last month, while in between stints—and parties—she'd spent close to three weeks living in Julia's condo.

Unlike Mari, Julia liked a quieter lifestyle, and wasn't into wild gatherings or casual one-night stands. But the truth was, taking the edge off herself always left her feeling alone, miserable, and in need of the real thing.

She'd spent so much time building her career, she rarely had time for a social life. She'd practically given up on the dating scene, and sometimes wondered if she really was just a jerk magnet.

Her sister was always attracted to successful, handsome men who doted on her—men Julia would love to date. Well, except for that self-centered soccer star from high school who had it all. Looks. Brains. Charisma.

The two were always joined at the hip, hanging at each other's houses and partying together after soccer games. Not that Julia was jealous. She wasn't. Not at all. And she certainly had no desire to live a day in her sister's shoes. Nope, not one little bit. What would she want with a well-known playboy like Chase Cooper, anyway? A guy who had never bothered to give her a second look. Well, except for the one time he'd caught her naked. Then again, he'd thought she was Mari, until she'd set him straight.

Julia let loose a long, slow breath and thought about the real reason guys never spared her a glance. She and Mari might look alike physically, but on the inside, they were completely different people. Julia was dubbed the smart, studious, dedicated sister and worked incredibly hard to get where she was. Mari, on the other hand, was labeled the talented and funny one. She was like a burst of sunshine to all those she touched. There was no denying that her vivacious and outgoing nature had helped play a significant part in her good fortune and plush job.

It was a cliché, Julia knew, but she'd grown up and lived in her sister's shadow long enough to understand the preconceived notions placed on twins. They'd both been stereotyped early on. Now, as a lawyer and a model, the two had gone on to fulfill those predetermined roles.

She read the invitation again. Could it have been meant for her? Whether it was or not, and no matter how tempting it sounded, she didn't have time to drop everything and fly halfway across the country to enjoy a week of R & R with some secret admirer, especially with the high-profile case going before the judge next week. She crinkled the invitation into a ball and tossed it into the trash. If it was for Mari, she was away at some exotic locale shooting a magazine cover and wouldn't be able to make it anyway. And if it was for her, well, she wasn't about to give it another thought.

• • •

Chase Cooper hadn't seen Mari Blair since high school, but it didn't take a whole lot of investigative work for his buddy Jag to discover that she was living in a downtown Halifax condo. Since he found no sign of a husband or children, Coop went forward with his plan to see if he could get her to the ranch — to discover if they could have a future together.

But as he finished securing his gelding in the end stall, he couldn't help but feel a bit anxious about their half-cocked plan. Nor could he help but question his logic as he casually strolled back toward the main lodge.

He took the stairs two at a time up to his private quarters at the far end of the lodge. Heading for the bathroom, he stripped off his sweat-dampened clothes, dropping them in a pile on the tiled floor. As he reached into the shower to turn on the water, his thoughts drifted to Julia Blair, but he shook his head to clear them. After inviting Mari to the ranch, the last person he should be thinking about was her quiet twin sister, the time he walked in on her naked, or how she informed Coop he wasn't her type.

Coop stepped into the shower and grabbed the soap. As he lathered his body, he tried to keep his thoughts on Mari. He recalled the time his group of friends went to Hubbard's Cove. Mari had stripped down that night and had invited Coop into the water with her. He could have gone for it, but never did. Contrary to what everyone thought, he and Mari had never dated, which went against high school protocol, considering he was the captain of the soccer team and she was head cheerleader. Still, they were pretty tight friends back in the day, climbing through each other's bedroom window to hang out or taking in the midnight show when no one else was around.

So why had he never asked her out? Because back then it wasn't Mari he was interested in. No, the truth was, he had it bad for her sister Julia. She ran in completely different circles and wouldn't give him the time of day. In fact, she seemed to despise him after he'd found her in Mari's closet naked. Even if she didn't hate him, there was nothing he could do about his attraction to her. Back in the day, he'd been best friends with her sister, which meant Julia was completely off-limits.

Hell, since getting close to Julia had been off the table, he should have just asked Mari out—to discover sooner rather than later if there could be something more between them. Instead he waited ten long years to do it. He'd never found anyone he enjoyed hanging out with more, which was why he and his two pals, Jag and Mac, had put together an asinine plan to fly the girls from their youth—the ones they thought had gotten away—to the ranch, to see if they could have a future.

He ran the soap over his body, hurrying to get ready before the plane arrived. As he soaped, his cock thickened. Only problem was that as he stroked himself, it wasn't Mari he was thinking about.

Shit. Shit. Shit.

He'd made a mistake asking Mari to come. He blasted the cold water, feeling less than comfortable about their upcoming reunion. He shouldn't be trying to turn his friendship with Mari into something more. Then again, maybe he'd get lucky and she wouldn't show.

Less than an hour later, all three guys stood beneath a towering maple tree. Ranch hands Tessa and Joel greeted the pilot of the small plane. When Joel opened the door for the passengers, the first to exit was Alix Harris—the girl Jag had invited.

Pacing beside Coop, Jag moaned as he took in Alix, the woman who'd plagued his dreams since high school. She shaded her inquisitive eyes from the blinding rays with her hand and glanced around, looking for someone she recognized.

The next to disembark was Jess Gray. Looking shy and somewhat timid, she hugged her bag tight to her chest and stepped up beside Alix. Her gaze flitted about uncomfortably, and she fidgeted with her hair, running the short chestnut strands around her index finger. Unable to control his enthusiasm, Mac stepped forward, and when Jess's glance caught his, a mixture of surprise and delight spread across her pretty face.

Unable to sit still, Coop paced around the tree and fisted and unfisted his hands. Would the girl from his past show? He honestly hoped not, because he never should have asked her to come. Sure, he'd been feeling a little played out, a little tired of going to bed with a girl only to wake up alone, lonely. But setting this plan in motion had been a huge mistake, one he and his friends never should have conspired over a few too many beers. His stomach tightened as he ran a shaky hand through his hair.

Two more passengers exited the plane, and after a long moment, he was fairly certain she hadn't come. A wave of relief rolled through him, and he drove his hands into his pockets. But when he spotted movement—long, slim legs descending the metal stairs—he swallowed hard, hoping that once he explained the situation to her, she'd simply laugh it off and they'd fall back into their easy friendship.

Thick dark hair cascaded over her slim shoulders as she stepped onto the tarmac and perused the unfamiliar surroundings. Coop's gaze leisurely roamed over her before his glance traveled back to her face. He took in the soft curve of her jaw, her tanned skin, and her full, lush lips. When her

glance met his and he drank in her come-hither whiskey
eyes—sultry and sensual beneath the summer sun—his jaw
dropped, hardly able to believe who he was staring at.

Well, holy shit...

Chapter Three

Holy shit...

Julia's stomach plummeted as she stared at the very familiar man lounging beneath the towering oak tree to the left of the tarmac—a handsome man she knew all too well and couldn't believe she was coming face-to-face with after all this time. At least this time she had her clothes on.

When his jaw dropped, understanding hit harder than a judge's wooden gavel. Her legs weakened, and moisture pebbled on her forehead as she realized what a colossal mistake she'd made.

Embarrassed and feeling like a complete and utter fool, Julia locked her knees to keep herself upright. She took a tentative step back, wishing the ground would open up and swallow her whole.

Good God, what the hell am I doing here?

With her mind spinning a million miles an hour, she berated herself for actually getting on the plane. But when she found out her case was no longer going to court, only to go home to see the invitation glaring at her from her garbage can, taunting her to go and see what this vacation was all about—and discover who had sent it—she went ahead and did just that.

She'd found herself maneuvering her car down the highway, heading toward the airport. As she drove, she worked to convince herself the short journey was for information purposes only—to discover the sender's true identity. Since impetuous behavior was completely out of character for her, she was pretty damn certain she wasn't going to step foot on the jumbo jet that took them to Alberta, or the small Cessna that just delivered them to the ranch—which was why she hadn't bothered with a suitcase.

But when she ran into Alix Harris and Jess Gray, two girls she recognized from high school, and they all stood around the gate and compared notes, curiosity got the better of her. Perhaps it was the lawyer in her, or perhaps it was the woman. Either way—luggage or not—she'd decided that, for once in her life, she was just going to act on impulse and see where the adventure led her.

And where it led her was straight to a dude ranch where the guy who'd seen her at her most vulnerable was standing in the shadows and likely waiting for her *sister*!

As her world tilted on its axis, the crowd dispersed, and she faltered backward. Her mind raced as the female ranch hand guided her off the small airstrip. She followed along numbly, forcing one leg in front of the other and wondering if she could jump back on the plane and get the hell out of Dodge before anyone realized the screwup. She turned at the sound of the engine roaring back to life, and sweat broke out on her skin when she spotted the small plane getting ready to taxi back down the short runway.

Feeling dizzy, she pinched her eyes shut, groping for something—anything—to grasp on to, when she felt a strong pair of arms slip around her waist to help balance her. She didn't have to turn around to know who those strong hands belonged to.

"You okay?"

Oh God, that voice. So deep. So sexy. So achingly familiar.

He tightened his grip, and she didn't dare open her eyes as she thought about those big, competent hands of his. Thought about how many times she had wished they were on her body, touching her, caressing her, making love to her. Her panties grew damp, and there wasn't a damn thing she could do to stifle the moan climbing from the depths of her dry throat.

Okay, so it was a lie. A complete and utter lie. She'd been jealous of Mari and Coop's relationship all along. And yes, she'd love to be wild and carefree like her sister for one day, mainly because it was the only way the boy from her fantasies was ever going to notice her. But he never bothered to give her the time of day before, which meant she was far better off without him in her life. Right?

So why then, after all these years, did his touch reduce her to a giddy schoolgirl? One who wanted him now as much as she ever did?

God, I am so pathetic!

Warm hands gripped her shoulders to spin her around. She opened her eyes and wished she hadn't. When her glance locked on his magnificent baby blues, there was no stopping her knees from wobbling. He pulled her closer until their groins meshed, and she could feel every striated muscle in his rock-hard body, specifically the one between his legs as it pressed against her.

She melted into his body, which could satisfy the most insatiable. What would it be like to have his work-roughened hands all over her, removing her clothes and touching her in the most erotic ways? Her lids fell shut as a myriad sinful thoughts tormented her suddenly overactive libido.

"Hey, are you okay?" he asked again.

His voice jostled her back to reality, and she remembered it was Mari he'd been waiting for under that oak tree, not her nerdy sister Julia. And the truth was, she wasn't about to offer herself to a man who didn't want her, no matter how much her body begged her to do just that.

Julia called on every ounce of strength she possessed, marshaled her wayward thoughts, and forced her voice to work, but for the first time in her life, words failed her. "I… uh…thirsty."

He gestured with a nod over his shoulder, and genuine concern laced his voice when he said, "Come on. It's scorching out here. Let's go inside for a cold drink."

Julia gave a quick shake of her head, and her voice came out far too breathy for her liking. "No. I should probably go."

Something that resembled heat flashed in his eyes, and it was all she could do to ignore the hunger bombarding her hormones. "Where?" he asked as they both watched the plane take to the sky. His sexy voice left her warm, wanting, and detesting him as much as she detested her traitorous body.

"Oh God," she croaked out.

As she stared into his bedroom blues, another shudder

ran through her, and she briefly wondered if she'd read him wrong. Maybe he didn't know the nerdy twin had boarded the plane. Then another more devious thought hit. If he didn't know, did she have it in her to pretend she was her sister? Just for one glorious week? Talk about the perfect opportunity to walk in her sister's shoes. As her mind warmed to the idea and her body stirred from his touch, she brushed her tongue over her lips and thought about where such a deceitful little lie would land her.

Right in his bed.

His perfect white teeth flashed as he smiled down at her. "Julia, are you okay?"

Okay, so much for that naughty plan. He obviously knew it was her. Too bad, really, because he was so damn hot.

No man should ever be allowed to look that good.

She extricated herself from his arms. Stalling, she brushed her hand over her blouse and form-fitting work skirt, smoothing out the wrinkles as she considered her next move. "Yeah, I'm just warm." She gave a casual shrug and decided to try to play off her unease. "I guess the invitation was meant for my sister."

Coop mimicked her easy shrug. "Yeah, but that's okay," he said lightly, a strange gleam in his eyes that piqued her interest. "You're here now, and I really want you to stay and enjoy yourself."

She studied his body language for movement—a skill she'd learned in law school; he was up to something. Crinkling her nose, she shaded the sun from her eyes and said, "Are there any car rentals around here?"

"Come on, Julia," he said. "You don't have to do that." He gave her a sexy, somewhat devious smile, and once again she couldn't help but wonder what was really going on here. Why had he invited Mari to the ranch after all these years? From what she knew, they'd lost touch after high school and Mari had been with many men since. The paparazzi loved to splash her face, and her antics, all over the rag mags. He likely wanted in on a little of the action. What other explanation could there be?

He gave a wide sweep of his hand. "You're welcome to stay as long as you like. I have a room ready for you and a week of fun planned."

"No, Coop," she corrected, his words hitting like a hard slap. "You have a room ready for my sister and a week of fun planned for her."

He frowned, and when he hooked his thumbs in his belt loops, Julia tried not to notice the way his jeans rode low on his hips. "I didn't mean — " he began.

She held her hand up to stop him. The last thing she wanted to hear was that he didn't mean that she, Julia Blair, could take over where her sister had left off. No, she really didn't want to hear that it wasn't her he wanted.

"It's okay. I need to get back anyway." She attempted a smile. "Especially since I boarded the plane on a whim and didn't even bring any luggage."

Coop went quiet for a long moment, and she wondered what was going through his mind. Finally, he broke the silence and said, "I'm not going to keep you here if you don't want to stay. There's another plane tomorrow at dinnertime. But until then you're kind of stuck." He stepped closer, his scent overwhelming her senses when he pitched his voice low and said, "Just don't make your decision until then, okay?"

"Why?"

"Because I think you might actually like it here." He held out his hand, and his grin turned mischievous when he started ticking things off on his fingers. "We've got a guest pool, great food, horses at your disposal, groomed riding trails…"

As he continued to list the amenities, Julia's gaze panned the estate and studied the old farmhouse, which had been restored to a quaint country inn. She took pleasure in the sight of the beautiful horses running inside the corral and the magnificent mountains off in the distance. It really was quite breathtaking.

"And, Julia."

She looked back at him. "Yeah?"

His eyes darkened, and his voice dropped an octave when he said, "I really am glad *you're* here."

Even though she didn't believe him, everything in the way he looked at her had her body trembling.

Must be the heat.

She shot another glance around the ranch. It was nice, and she didn't have much of a choice.

"So what do you say?"

She gave a resigned sigh, but deep down couldn't deny that she was a bit excited by the prospect of hanging out at the dude ranch. The thought of being on a horse again was very alluring. She'd just be sure to keep her distance from Coop until the plane came back to rescue her.

After a quick consultation with herself, she answered with, "I guess if I'm stuck here for the night, then I might as well enjoy the place."

He flashed a wide grin. "Good. Come on. And I'm sure I can find spare clothes for you." He grabbed her hand and pulled, and she wished he'd stop being so considerate and sweet. It made it too hard to hate him. "You look to be about the same size as Tessa."

She wondered who Tessa was, but resisted the urge to ask. Instead, she noted the way he'd angled his head to get a better glimpse of her. She could feel his eyes studying her, taking in her navy pencil skirt, starched white blouse, and sensible pumps. She felt completely out of place standing next to this sexy, laid-back cowboy. Then again, they'd always traveled in different circles.

"What?" she asked and shifted uncomfortably under his scrutinizing gaze.

"I was just wondering."

"Wondering what?"

"What exactly is it that you need to hurry back for?"

She thought long and hard before answering. "Nothing now, I guess," she said honestly, having no reason to lie to him, other than the fact that she didn't want him to know her life was as boring as her clothes, and that unlike her twin sister, Julia Blair was all work and no play. But he probably already knew that.

She kept pace with his long strides as they walked the gravel path to the ranch. "Then why didn't you pack?"

Julia adjusted her purse over her shoulder. "I wasn't planning on coming."

"Then why did you go to the airport?"

She gave an uneasy laugh, and instead of telling him that her curiosity got the better of her, she said, "I don't remember you being a man of so many questions."

He gave her a crooked sideways grin that fluttered her heart, not to mention other parts of her body.

"So what do you remember about me?" he asked as he hurried his steps, moving ahead of her slightly.

Everything.

From his gorgeous body and handsome, boyish face to the way he played the field, and she wasn't talking about the soccer field. All the girls had lusted after him while she watched from the sidelines.

"Nothing," she lied.

"Good."

Julia arched a curious brow. "Good? Why good?"

His mouth turned up at the corner, and his sexy smile warmed her right to the tips of her toes. "Because I was a bit of a cocky prick back in the day, don't you think?"

"I hadn't noticed." The truth was, he might have been self-centered, out for his own pleasure like every other teen boy she knew, but he did have qualities that drew her to him. That day he'd found her in the closet, it might have hurt her feelings when he said he would never want to walk in on her naked, but he'd been a gentleman, respectful, and went to lengths to protect her from his friends. Rumor had it that later that night, he kicked the shit out of Jag and Mac for laughing at her.

"Maybe that's because you were too busy studying," he said, which raised the question, what did he remember about her?

As she took pleasure in the sight of his hard body, she noticed the new crook of his nose—how did he break it? Her gaze left his face to take in broad shoulders that tapered to a trim waist, long, hard legs, and a gorgeous ass that looked so damn good in his worn, low-riding jeans.

When his hand tightened over hers, his rough calluses

scraped against her palms, there was nothing she could do to ignore the tremble moving through her.

As they approached the front entrance of the lodge, she was about to ask what he remembered about her, but he moved close, too close. Her brain stalled, and her body temperature ramped up a few degrees

He dipped his head, and for a moment she thought he was moving in for a kiss. He tipped his hat, pulled open the heavy door, and in a sexy drawl that nearly had her melting like a summertime Popsicle, said, "After you, ma'am."

Rattled by his close proximity and overwhelming ruggedness, she berated herself for her foolish thoughts. Of course he wasn't moving in for a kiss. She forced herself to grin at his playfulness. Careful not to touch him, she walked into what appeared to be a replica of a nineteenth-century saloon.

The cool interior helped push back the heat, not to mention the lust, and cleared her head. She glanced around the nearly empty watering hole and smiled as she took note of the decor. Coop tipped his hat to the woman behind the counter.

"I'll have a beer," he said, and turned to Julia. "What would you like?"

Julia swallowed, and even though she wasn't much of a drinker, she looked at the draft tap and was sure she could use a cold one right about now. "Same," she answered.

Coop pulled a chair out for her. Who knew he'd grow up to be such a gentleman? Well, maybe she did. He straddled the seat to her left, and she glanced around. How did Coop and his two best buds end up on a dude ranch?

She'd recognized Mac and Jag. What were the three of

them up to? They had caused enough trouble in high school to last a lifetime, but obviously, they were up to their old antics. Why else would they have gifted her—well, her sister—and the other two girls with an all-expense-paid vacation to the ranch? They were obviously living out some wild, youthful fantasy.

God, would the three hellions ever grow up?

Coop adjusted his hat on his head, and she watched the muscles along his arm tighten.

She cleared her throat. "A cowboy, huh?" Julia asked.

"Yeah, when the mood strikes."

She wasn't quite sure what he meant by that, but when he didn't bother to elaborate, she said in a low voice, more to herself than to him, "I never would have thought."

"I guess you never know what kind of curveball life is going to throw at you."

He had a strange, vulnerable look in his eye. What had been thrown his way? What events led Coop here, to a dude ranch in the middle of nowhere? Because quite honestly, she'd never taken him for a ranch kind of guy. But she guessed he'd simply taken his playboy antics from the soccer field to the corral. Heck, what girl didn't love a cowboy, right? There certainly wasn't anything wrong with such a profession. It was a respectable job, but in senior year she overheard him talking about a career in sports medicine.

The waitress came with their drinks, and Julia took a big gulp and placed her frosty mug on the table before her. The cool liquid went down so nice and smooth that she continued to drink until she quenched her thirst. When she began to feel the effects of the alcohol—compliments of an empty stomach—she sipped slower and inched back on her chair to let loose a long, slow breath. Truthfully, until she stepped into this saloon, she hadn't realized just how tightly wound she'd been.

The place was nice, comfortable, and designed to put its patrons at ease. After working hard for the last few months, perhaps a night at the ranch was just the thing she needed. Too bad she couldn't stay longer. Sure, Coop had put the offer on the table, but she was intelligent enough to know that he was just being polite, trying to salvage a bad situation and make the best of it. He didn't really want *her* here.

"I never took you for a beer-drinking kind of girl." Coop gestured to the waitress for another, and Julia fought down the burst of heat creeping toward her face when she noticed that her mug was nearly empty.

Trying for casual, she said, "There's probably a lot you don't know about me."

He leaned toward her, and his mouth was so close that if she inched forward their lips would be touching. "So where should we start?" he asked.

"Why should we bother?"

"Why shouldn't we?"

She really didn't have a good answer for that. When she didn't respond, he continued. "So what do you do for a living, Julia?" She was taken aback by his question, as well as the genuine interest in his eyes. She really thought he'd spend the night grilling her on Mari, and was actually a little shocked that he wanted to know more about her. She decided to play along, since she had nothing else to do and nowhere else to be.

"I'm a lawyer," she said, and waited for his eyes to glaze over. When they widened with interest, it caught her off guard.

He gave a slow nod. "Beauty and brains," he murmured, giving a slow appreciative nod. "I'm not surprised, really. You always were smart."

He thinks I'm beautiful? Probably just being nice.

She sat there staring at him, taking in the thoughtfulness on his face, and strangely enough, the admiration in his eyes when he spoke about her didn't make her feel that she was being judged. As a teen, she'd shied away from such blatant observations, hating that she was the smart one and her sister was the fun one, but this time, she could feel a measure of pride welling up inside her.

"My turn," Julia said, no longer wanting to talk about herself.

He gave a mock shiver. "Let the interrogation…er…I mean questions begin."

"First, let me say that you weren't always a prick. I remember the time you saved Davy Brown from the bullies." Julia wasn't sure why she'd brought up that particular incident. Maybe it was that vulnerable look she'd spotted in his eyes when he talked about life and its curveballs, or maybe it was because that was the day she'd fallen for him.

He gave her a coy look and teased, "I thought you said you didn't remember anything about me."

"Well, maybe I remembered a few things." He gave her a knowing grin. "But there are still a few things I'd like to know."

He leaned forward until their knees bumped under the table, and he pitched his voice low when he asked, "What do you want to know, Julia?"

Her heart lurched at the deep, suggestive tone of his

voice. And oh, the way he said her name. How would it sound whispered against her lips as he made love to her? She shifted in her chair, crossed her legs against the pressure building between them at the thought.

Clearing her throat she asked, "Why a dude ranch?"

He got quiet for a moment, then gave a light shrug and leaned into her, his breath warm on her face. "Isn't it every boy's dream to grow up to be a cowboy?"

She noticed the careful way he sidestepped giving her a direct answer, but for some inexplicable reason, the lawyer in her—or maybe it was the woman—wanted to know.

"Yes, but most don't go on to realize the dream. So why this old ranch? Why here?" She paused to wave her hand around. "In the middle of nowhere."

She expected him to come back with some smart-ass comment about getting the girls, but when he sat back, lowered his head, and frowned, his guard slipped slightly. Her heart tightened. This was something personal. Someone or something had hurt him. She always thought of him as such a happy-go-lucky guy. Humor disappeared from his eyes as turbulent waves of emotion rolled across his face. He quickly tamped them down, cleared his throat, and smiled, his guard firmly back in place.

Returning to playful mode, he looked at her pointedly and flashed his perfect white teeth in a smile. "It was the right thing at the right time." He grabbed his glass and held it up to her, but this time his smile didn't quite reach his eyes. "Now come on. Here's to friends. Old and new."

She clinked glasses with him, appreciating how smoothly he evaded certain questions and redirected the conversation. Clearly, he was keeping something from her. Not that he owed her any details—he didn't—but she still couldn't help but wonder what these guys were up to.

The lawyer in her itched to dig deep to get to the bottom of matters, and oddly enough, the woman in her wanted to take him into her arms and kiss the truth free. Which one would win?

Chapter Four

Julia paced around the bedroom and looked at the stack of clothes on her bed. The elderly gentleman manning the front desk had delivered them a few moments ago. Cursing herself for not having the foresight to pack her own bag, even though she swore she wasn't going to board the plane, she sifted through the pile of clothes until she found a silky white nightgown.

After pulling it on, she padded softly around the room, running her hands over the quilted bedspread, the oak night table, and the small corner desk until she stood before her window. The warm evening breeze ruffled her short gown, and the cool silk felt gloriously soft against her skin. As it caressed her flesh, her nipples tightened in response. But she suspected it had more to do with Coop than the night air.

Earlier in the afternoon, Coop had jumped up from the table and guided her outside. He took her on a long walk around the ranch, giving her a personal tour of the facilities, and introduced her to the horses before he treated her to a hearty ranch dinner. After the meal, she found herself alone in her rustic, cozy room. One minute she'd been enjoying apple cobbler with Coop, and the next, the pretty brunette Tessa had come along to drag him away.

Of course, his sudden departure had been for the best. While she might have been enjoying his company—maybe a little too much—she wasn't here to exchange intimacies with the sexy cowboy, no matter how delicious that sounded. No, she was only overnighting it at the ranch until the plane came back to rescue her. But that still didn't stop her from thinking about where he'd rushed off to in such a hurry.

Groaning out loud and determined to get him out of her mind, she spun around and examined her bed. After a long day traipsing across the country, she knew she should just crawl between the sheets and try to get a good night's sleep. But her body felt achy, needy, her insides far too fired up to settle in for the night.

Damn you, Coop.

She twisted back toward her window and drew open the thin sheer curtain to take in the magnificent view of the mountains. She perused the wide expanse of horse country, noting the huge homestead at the far end of the ranch and the small cedar cottage nestled at the foot of the mountain as she inhaled the fragrant scents. Then, catching her by surprise, Coop exited the quaint cottage.

Noting the tension in his posture, the stiffness in his every step, she watched him until he disappeared from her line of sight. Once he was gone, her gaze strayed back to the well-kept chalet with the cedar siding, painted shutters, and wraparound deck.

Was it Tessa's quarters?

Hating the direction of her thoughts—after all, she had no right to feel jealous—she drew back from the window and threw herself onto her bed. She closed her eyes and willed herself to sleep, but her lids sprang open when a soft knock sounded on her door.

"Who is it?" She threw her legs over the side of her mattress and angled her head, listening to the quiet response coming from the hallway.

"It's me," Coop whispered. "I just wanted to check in on you and make sure you have everything you need."

At the concern in Coop's voice, Julia flicked on her lamp and walked to the door. She opened it slightly and peeked out, noticing the deep worry lines beneath his eyes. Something happened at the chalet, something that had upset him.

Unease settled in the pit of her stomach. "Coop, is everything okay?"

Without giving any thought to her skimpy sleepwear, she pulled her door open wider. When his eyes dropped from her face to her body—her breasts to be specific—it occurred to her that he could see her every curve through the transparent silk, especially with her lamp backlighting her frame.

The worry instantly disappeared from his eyes, and when want moved in to take its place, a warm, needy shudder raced down her spine. As her body came alive, she quickly gave him a once-over. Everything from the hot, hungry way he looked at her to the heat she felt emanating off his rock-hard body turned her inside out. She felt exposed, unsure.

Desired.

Coop raked his hands through his hair, mussing the short

dark strands until he looked warm and sexy, as though he'd just crawled out of bed. His overwhelmingly rugged good looks set her body on fire, and she nearly forgot that she wasn't the one he really wanted.

"I…uh…I just wanted to make sure Benjamin had stopped by to deliver a few of Tessa's clothes and make sure they fit." A short pause and then, "But…I…uh…I can see — "

What he can see is my entire naked body! Again!

Julia wrapped her arms around her chest, positioned herself behind the door, and tried to sound casual when she said, "He did. Thank you for that. And please, thank Tessa, too. You were right. We are the same size." Okay, now she was just rambling like an idiot, but as he stood there looking at her as if he wanted to eat her alive, she couldn't seem to help herself. She was completely out of her comfort zone.

Coop nodded. "So, ah, I'll see you in the morning then."

She returned his nod, thinking it might be best if she never set eyes on him again. The man had trouble written all over him, and if she spent any more time with him, she just might do something she would only regret later, like rope him and tie him to her bed until sunup, a week from tomorrow.

• • •

As Coop tossed and turned in his bed, early-morning light filtering in through his curtains, he couldn't settle his mind enough to sleep. He punched his pillow, completely fired up that Julia was here.

Jesus Christ.

Julia was here.

On the ranch.

With him.

He wasn't sure he'd ever be able to wrap his brain around this unexpected turn of events.

She might have been off-limits before, but goddammit, they weren't in high school anymore, and this time he was going to go for it. To show her that it was the best damn mix-up to ever happen and just how happy he was that it was *her* who boarded that plane. He was determined to convince her to stay, and by the end of the week, she'd damn well know *she* was the one he'd always wanted.

Coop turned his focus to the morning chores ahead of him, hoping to get them done so he could spend the rest of his time with Julia. He climbed from his bed, pulled on his jeans, and walked to his window. After a very restless night, he stretched out his tired body and drew back his curtain to expose the distant peaks and his own private view of the back pasture.

At the crest of the mountain, warm fingers of golden light clawed at the fading black as dawn began its approach. Coop smiled, hoping to get in a good hard swim in the staff's private mineral pond at the far end of the ranch. He was the only one who ever used it. The others felt it was too much trouble to get to, but he found the trek invigorating and well worth the peaceful solitude once he reached it. Some mornings he just sat there and watched the sunrise before his swim. Other times, at the end of a long day working the ranch, then an even longer night caring for his mom, he'd sit for a while in the soothing water and let it work its magic on his work-worn body and if only for a moment, wash away the pain of watching his mother slowly slip away.

As he enjoyed the magnificent view, Coop raked his ruffled hair off his forehead. He hadn't seen Jag or Mac since the plane arrived late yesterday afternoon. He hoped things were going as well for the two of them as they were for him.

A movement down by the water caught his attention. He squinted against the rising sun and wondered which guest would be up and about at the crack of dawn, and what were they doing in the ranch's "off-limits" area. All available facilities were laid out in the brochure, and that particular pond wasn't one of them. He opened his window, and the fresh scent of hay wafted before his nostrils as he leaned out for a better look. The distant sight of a woman stripping her clothes off and climbing into the water set his heart galloping and his mind racing.

Julia.

He pushed away from the window and ran to the edge of the ranch. Less than five minutes later, Coop stood at the embankment, mesmerized by the erotic vision before him. Waves splashed against the grassy shore, while creamy white skin and soft, sexy curves surfaced, only to disappear again beneath the glistening water. His skin grew hot, and his cock thickened inside his unforgiving jeans.

An odd sensation, one he'd never felt before, built inside his chest as he watched her play in his pool. What the hell was it? Possessiveness? As he mulled that over, Julia stood. Thigh-deep in the pond, she faced the mountain and tossed her hair over her shoulders, spraying water in the air. He'd never seen such a beautiful vision. His heart missed a beat as longing filled him. As her hair fell low on her back, his gaze followed it down, right to damp panties that showcased a lovely, heart-shaped ass.

Jesus.

Dressed in nothing but her bra and underwear, she lifted her arms over her head and began stretching out her body. Beads of water trickled down her creamy flesh, and when they dipped inside her pretty white panties, it was all Coop could do to keep a coherent thought.

A low growl of longing sounded deep in his throat, and there wasn't a damn thing he could do to stifle it. As the sound pierced the quiet of the morning, Julia spun around, her big brown eyes wide, her mouth agape.

"Sorry, didn't mean to startle you," Coop said quickly, struggling to avert his gaze when all he wanted to do was look his fill. She was so goddamn beautiful, perfect really, that it was almost impossible to look away. But she deserved privacy, so he turned. "This area is off-limits, and I didn't expect to find anyone here."

"I didn't…I thought—"

"It's okay. I don't mind."

"I didn't have a suit," she rushed out. "So I came here where I could swim and exercise in private."

"Really, Julia, it's okay. I don't mind at all. In fact…" He stopped himself before he said something to scare her off, something like, *In fact, I'd like to climb in there with you and trail my tongue over your entire body until you're screaming for me to fuck you.*

But he knew she was unsure of this whole situation, and he had to take it slow. The last thing he wanted to do was scare her off and ruin his chance at having something amazing with her.

"In fact what?" she asked, her tone soft, sensual.

He rocked back and forth on his feet, the sound of the

water lapping against her naked flesh filling him with lust and urging him to turn back around to see her. His muscles bunched, and he stared at the lodge in the distance as he struggled to answer her. "I…just…ah…wanted…"

"You just what?" she asked, pushing him for an answer, a reminder that she was a lawyer and wasn't about to let him get off so easily.

When he didn't answer, she said, "Coop."

His pulse kicked up at the soft, sexy way she said his name.

Was it possible…?

Could she be flirting with him?

Before he realized what he was doing, he spun back around to face her. When their eyes met and locked, he didn't miss the way her smoky gaze left his face to take in his chest, his stomach, the bulge between his legs. As her blatant perusal paused on his growing erection, he damn near lost all sense of control and climbed in there with her.

That was desire in her eyes, hunger brewing just below the surface. His heart raced, and his body tightened.

"Well," she probed. "What did you want, Coop?"

Goddammit, the look in her eyes and the raw ache of lust he heard in her voice spoke volumes. She wanted him every bit as much as he wanted her, and that made him the happiest fucking guy in the world.

Everything about this sweet and sexy woman weakened his resolve, and he knew he wanted her more than ever.

The hell with taking it slow.

Unhinged at the want reflecting in her eyes, he hungered for her with an intensity that scared the shit out of him. As blood pounded through his veins, Coop dipped his head and took one step closer, deciding a blatant seduction was most definitely in order.

"I was wondering if you'd like some company."

Dark lashes slowly blinked over whiskey-brown eyes, but when they opened, something came over her face, something that filled him with unease. With a frown marring her forehead, she folded her arms over her chest, dipped lower in the water, and said, "I think you've got the wrong girl."

Chapter Five

Julia stared at Coop's retreating back, her stomach plummeting. What the hell had she been thinking?

While she wanted to say yes to his proposition—God knew her body was urging her to invite him in and go for it—his sexy offer had suddenly reminded her that it was Mari he really wanted. Hurt caused her to strike out at him.

The second those blunt words had left her mouth, Coop backed off, his eyes dark, confused. And why wouldn't he be confused? It was clear to anyone within a fifty-mile radius that her entire body had reacted with want when she first caught him watching her.

And she'd turned him away.

God, I am such an idiot.

Wasn't this the perfect opportunity to live a day in her sister's life? Was she really going to pass that up?

Okay, so Julia might not have been the one Coop had been expecting to get off that plane, but maybe this wasn't about him anymore. Maybe this moment was about her and what she wanted.

She walked from the pond, quickly towel-dried her body, and pulled on a borrowed pair of denim shorts and a pretty pink T-shirt that was a little too snug around her breasts. Once dressed, she followed the path Coop had taken and soon found him alone inside the barn, the warm morning light drifting in through the open doors and falling over his hard body.

He had his back to her, and she watched the way he quietly talked to his horse, the way he stroked the gelding with care. While Coop might be tough and rugged on the outside, there was a reflective side of him, a side that was sweet and caring. A side that always tugged at her, and drew her in.

"Coop," she said, trying not to sound breathless as she imagined those capable hands of his on her body, taking her to places she'd never before been.

He spun around to face her, and when his glance met hers, he raked shaky hands through his hair. "Julia," he began. "Jesus, I'm sorry. I misread—"

She took a deep breath and blurted out, "You're not the one at fault here."

He cast his eyes downward. "I made a mistake—"

"No, you didn't. I did."

His gaze flew back to hers, and he hooked his thumbs through his belt loops in a familiar move. She tried not to re-act when the hard muscles along his arms flexed and relaxed again. "What are you talking about? I shouldn't have—"

"Yes, you should have."

He gave a slow shake of his head. "I don't understand."

Julia drew a centering breath, and while she couldn't

pretend to be her sister, it didn't mean that she couldn't act like her and get what she wanted from Coop, what she always wanted. She went up on her toes and said, "The answer is yes, Coop."

She watched his throat work as he swallowed. "Yes?"

"Yes, I would like some company." She stepped into him, and when she aligned her body with his, positioning herself against his cock, he slid his arm around her waist, tugging her against him.

His gaze moved over her face, assessing her. The heat from his body, as well as the hardness between his legs, excited her. Made her feel bold and adventurous.

He dipped his head, his mouth closer to hers. "Are you sure?"

No. She had no idea what she was doing, but she appreciated his concern nonetheless. He was easy to trust, easy to be with, and she wanted to spend the next few hours doing it the cowboy's way.

She put her hands on his shoulders and looked his body over as she let them slide down his chest. "I want this," she murmured. "All of this."

He exhaled sharply, and his hands shook as they trailed up her back. He smiled at her, but it wasn't dark or predatory. It was soft, sexy…tempting.

He touched her damp hair, and her thoughts stalled as he seductively wound a long strand between his fingers. Her insides quivered with the needy way he looked at her. God, no man had ever looked at her like that before.

His gaze dropped to the two wet spots on her T-shirt. His Adam's apple bobbed. "You're all wet."

Oh God, he had no idea.

He backed her up, and she could feel a new urgency in his touch, one that excited her beyond anything she'd ever known.

God, was this really happening? After all these years was she really going to touch Coop, feel him touch her in return?

"A girl should have what she wants," he said, his voice dripping with promise.

Her nipples tightened with arousal, and everything inside her urged her to go for it—to enjoy a wild ride with this sexy cowboy before returning to Nova Scotia, to the real world where she was all work and no play.

When they hit the wall, his groin bumped hers, and a moan of want crawled out of her throat. Coop grabbed her hands and pinned them above her head. As he caged her between his chest and the wooden slats, her entire body tightened in anticipation.

Coop must have misread her reactions. He positioned his mouth close to hers, and his voice came out a little breathless, a little labored, when he said, "I'll stop if you want me to. But Jesus, if you're having second thoughts, please let me know now before—"

"I don't want you to stop."

He exhaled sharply. "No regrets?" he asked, his warm breath whispering across her quivering flesh.

She gestured with a slight nod, answering his question. "Are we going to go back—?"

His voice dropped an octave as he spread her legs with his knee. His expression was tender and hot when he said, "No, I want you right here, right now."

When her body pulsed in anticipation, Coop groaned out loud. She moved her hips. The movement was slight, but highly suggestive. "Then what are you waiting for?" she asked, hardly able to believe how bold she felt and how much she liked it.

His lips closed over hers. His kiss was hard, hot, and so damn hungry that it curled her toes and shut down her ability to think with any clarity. Which was fine by her, really. Because at the moment, she didn't want to think. She wanted to feel, to concentrate on this hot man and the pleasure he was offering.

And by God, he had so much pleasure to offer…

His tongue moved inside to play with hers, and she reveled in the minty flavor of his mouth. Her heart crashed, and as he deepened the kiss, it took every ounce of strength she possessed to keep her knees from failing. She'd never wanted a man as much as she did him. His hands slid over her, and she shook, needing him to hurry this along before she burst into a million tiny pieces.

As if he read her thoughts, he put his hands on her waist to support her and spun her around to face the ladder leading to the loft above. He nudged her to set her in to motion, and put his mouth near her ear when they reached it.

"Climb," he commanded, and reached into his saddlebag to grab something.

She started up, and he stayed close behind. Hyperaware her backside was inches from his face, she hurried up. She reached the top, and Coop gave her an easy shove until she was sprawled out on a pile of hay. Coop stood over her, his gaze leisurely trailing over her body as though he was savoring the sight of her—savoring this moment. She rolled her tongue around a suddenly dry mouth.

"Now this is where I want you," he murmured, the fire in

his eyes licking at her flesh.

The dark intensity in his gaze did the strangest things to her body. Julia gulped air and moistened her lips the best she could as goose bumps broke out on her flesh.

"You shouldn't do that." Coop dropped to his knees, widened her thighs, and positioned himself there.

"What?"

God, she couldn't believe how rugged and sexy he looked as he slid himself between her legs. A warm breeze blew through the loft, and she caught a hint of Coop's rich scent stirring in the air. As it stimulated her senses, she ached for him in a way she'd never ached for a man before.

"Your lips," he murmured, his lusty gaze zeroing in on her mouth. "You shouldn't lick them like that."

Rational thought fled when Coop dragged his hands over her thighs, his sexy gaze roaming over her face. With her body taking over where her brain had left off, her throat tightened and her flesh heated with unbridled want.

Breathing was difficult. "Why…why not?"

"Because it makes me crazy, that's why."

"And?" She licked her lips again, wanting to make him as wild as he was making her.

He groaned, crawled up her body, and then tangled his fingers through her hair before pushing it off her face.

"Cut it out or I'll lose it," he growled into her ear. "And I'm not ready to. Not yet. Not with you."

When she heard the need—the urgency—in his voice, her heart began racing. She loved that she had this effect on him. "Why not?"

A muscle in his jaw twitched. "Because now that I've got you where I want you, I'm not in a hurry to go anywhere. I plan to take my sweet time with you, Julia. I plan to make you scream for me."

"Coop." Anticipation quaked through her.

His mouth curved as he traced her lips with his index finger. With a bemused expression on his handsome face, he lowered his voice and in a sexy drawl said, "I take it you like that idea."

"Yeah. I...I like it a lot." She was surprised she could even find her voice as his mouth came closer and closer to hers.

The second his lips closed over hers, her body sizzled, and she was certain she'd died and gone to heaven. Or maybe it was hell. Either way, she didn't care. His kisses told her the journey was going to be worth it.

His hands trailed over her curves, his rough calluses scraping along her skin and leaving a quiver in their wake. He gripped the hem of her T-shirt and tugged it up and over her head. His thumbs went to her wet bra, and a tortured look came over his face.

He stroked her nipples through the white lace, and his touch sent shock waves rocketing through her.

"Last night," he murmured in the hollow of her throat, his scalding lips firing her blood, "when I came to your room. It was all I could do not to drag you to this loft and take you."

"I...me..."

He lifted his head. "What? Were you thinking the same?" He briefly shut his eyes. "If you tell me you were thinking the same I could very well lose it."

"I was," she said.

"Christ." He wet his lips, pulled the cups from her

breasts, and drew her hard bud into his mouth. He groaned, swiping his hot tongue over her achy nipples. "So sweet, so fucking sweet."

Julia ran her hands though his hair, holding him to her. His touch burned right to her core, and she could feel small quakes pulling at her. Jesus, no man had ever made her come simply from kissing her breasts before. Then again, none of those men were Chase Cooper.

As his breath scorched her, she writhed beneath him, aching for his touch. He paid homage to her other breast, and when he bit down, air ripped from her lungs.

He lifted his head, a sheepish look on his face. "Sorry...I just..." He exhaled, his warm breath fell over her. "Well, I did warn you."

A thrill raced through her, and she slid her hands around his head to guide him back. A chuckle sounded in his throat, and with the soft blade of his tongue, he soothed the sting. The combination of pain and pleasure was almost more than she could bear.

Once he had his fill of her breasts, he trailed his tongue down her body until he reached the button on her shorts. Making quick work of that barrier, he pulled down her zipper and dragged her shorts and panties to her ankles.

After she kicked them off, he settled back on his knees and sat there, taking his sweet time to stare at her nakedness. She reached for him, her body achy, needy, but when she caught the raw ache of lust in his eyes, she trembled from head to toe.

"Coop," she choked out.

He gripped her legs, spread them wide, and then leaned into her, his breath scorching her flesh. His burning mouth pressed hungrily to her heat while he brushed the soft pad of his thumb over her inflamed clit.

He moaned in pure bliss, and the warmth of his mouth as he feasted on her just about pushed her over the precipice. God, she'd never been so responsive before, but everything in the way this man touched her turned her on. Never had she felt so wild, so sexy…so wanted.

As his tongue seared her, her muscles clenched. She could feel need building, coming to a peak. When a tremor raced through her, he pressed deeper, his mouth taking full possession of her sex. He licked, sucked, nibbled, and stroked, the rough velvet of his tongue making her delirious. Past the point of no return, she cried out his name, just as he had said she would.

"Yes," she screamed, giving no regard to anyone or anything but this moment and this man. A horse may have whinnied, but she couldn't be certain.

"You taste so fucking good," he murmured. When he urged her thighs wider apart, granting himself deeper access, a whimper escaped her lips.

He applied more pressure to her aching nub, and she began moving, pressing against his mouth, her body seeking what it needed. Coop inserted a finger, and then slowly drew it out, only to push it back in again. She grew slicker and slicker with each thrust. In no time at all, her body pulsed and throbbed with the hot flow of release. Heat swept through her, her climax so damn intense she had to grip his shoulders to hang on.

"That's so good."

Every muscle in her body tightened in euphoria, and pure ecstasy reverberated through her blood. He brushed his tongue over her clit in low, lazy strokes that drew out her orgasm until her very last spasm.

She tried to pull him to her, but he wasn't done with her. Instead of crawling up her body or urging her to tend to his physical needs like every other man she'd been with, he stayed deep between her legs.

God, she'd never had a man give without taking before. He pushed another finger deep inside her for a deliciously snug fit.

A second orgasm hit fast and furious, and when her walls closed around him, his head came up and he growled out loud. As she watched him take such joy in pleasuring her, her entire body trembled from want, from so many years of longing for this man. She exhaled a shallow breath and grabbed his shoulders tighter, desperate to feel him inside her.

"Please…"

"Please what?"

She exhaled a shaky breath, impatience thrumming through her. "I want you. Inside me."

"Soon," he murmured, but she knew by his voice and the tension in his body that he was every bit as crazed as she was.

"No. I've waited too long for this, wanted you for too long. I need you inside me. Now." She was so delirious with want she had no idea what she was saying, but Coop must have understood, because something warm and possessive passed over his eyes. Hot lust shimmered in the depth of his baby blues as he crawled up her body, the glorious weight of his hard torso pressing down on hers.

His hands settled on either side of her as he brushed his

lips over hers. A second later, he was removing his pants and pulling a condom out of his jeans to roll it on. Looking a bit rattled and frantic, he settled himself back on top of her, the tip of his thick cock teasing her.

"Tell me you want this."

She swallowed, her entire body quaking. "I think you know I do."

His nostrils flared, and there was a new intensity about him when he said, "Tell me you want me."

"I want you, Coop."

As soon as the words left her mouth, he slid his fingers through her hair and plunged deep, spreading her walls as he pushed his impressive girth inside her.

She wrapped her arms around him and held tight, knowing she was in for the ride of a lifetime. When he began pumping, their bodies coming together as though they were made for each other, the pleasure was almost too much for her to bear. She vibrated in delight, and when he angled his body for deeper thrusts, her low moan curled around them.

"You're so tight, baby. So fucking tight."

She shuddered, every nerve ending coming alive as another wave hit her hard. Her muscles pulsed.

He growled and closed his eyes. "You're killing me here, sweetheart." Coop pushed harder, his hands fisting her hair as he buried his mouth in the crook of her neck. "But it's too soon…"

He lifted his head, and when she saw how desperate he was, Julia cupped his face. "It's not too soon. Please."

When some deeper emotion flashed in the stormy depths of his eyes, her breath caught.

"Coop?" she asked.

"I...I'm good," he panted. "It's just...I can't believe you're here with me."

With that, he began slamming hard, frantic, like a man starved for so much more than just physical release. As he ravished her, she welcomed each thrust, met each push with one of her own.

Never wanting the moment to end, she raked her hands over his back, her sex squeezing his cock. In no time at all, his body tightened, his muscles clenched, and then he stilled. He threw his head back, and his cock throbbed as he came.

Once he stopped pulsing, he dropped down on top of her, moisture sealing their bodies together, and whispered, "Next time I'll go slower, baby. I promise."

Next time?

As she lay there beneath him, cloaked in contentment from the best sex she'd ever had, she exhaled a shaky breath. She wasn't sure what to say, or how to tell him there wasn't going to be a next time. This was a one-shot deal, and soon the plane would be coming to collect her.

She opened her mouth to speak, but Coop pressed his fingers to her lips to hush her. Someone had entered the barn. She heard voices, along with the creak of hinges as the stall doors opened.

With Coop on top of her, his hard body pressing down on hers in the most erotic ways, they remained quiet. As his gaze roamed over her face, she realized how much she liked him on top of her, how much she'd like to spend the rest of the day trapped beneath his hardness.

He smiled at her, a naughty grin that turned her inside out and reminded her that she never, ever did wild things like this. But by God, she sure was glad she gave in to her urges and stepped out of her comfort zone. Coop was warm, sexy, and wild, and no man had ever been so crazed, so frantic with her before. Being here with him like this was pretty much the highlight of her life.

Her hands went to his face. She traced his cheek, his jaw, and then the crook of his nose. Again, she wondered how he'd broken it.

They stayed quiet for a good twenty minutes. Until the guests saddled their horses and left the barn. It was only when they were alone again that Coop rolled off her, but instead of climbing to his feet, he moved in close and gently pressed his lips to hers. As his tender kiss took her by surprise, weird and wonderful emotions blossomed inside her. Except in this erotic fantasy with the man from her past, emotions weren't allowed.

Needing to get her head on straight and remind herself this was just casual sex, they had no future together, she wiggled out from underneath him and asked, "Am I keeping you from your chores?"

He grinned. "Nope, but I'm keeping you from yours."

She crinkled her nose. "Ah, I have chores?"

In a teasing drawl, he said, "This is a working dude ranch. Did you think you were going to get off so easily?" He dragged the words "get off" out slowly.

"I kind of just did," she returned, teasing him back.

Her voice drifted off when something in his expression changed. Gone was his playful look, replaced by one full of dark intensity as he lazily trailed a finger over her nose, mouth, and throat.

He angled his head, his eyes moving over her face. "You do plan on staying the week, don't you?"

"I didn't…I wasn't…"

As she worked to formulate a clear response, he brushed his mouth over hers, and a warm shiver of need pulsed in her body. Her mind raced. If a day acting more like her care-free sister was this amazing, what would a week be like? But would she be able to do it? Would she be able to live life on the wild side and keep her emotions out of it?

"Well?" he asked.

"I don't—"

"Maybe you're in need of more convincing," he teased, sliding back over her.

Chapter Six

As Coop sat across from Julia at the breakfast table, he couldn't stop smiling. The sex had been good, quite possibly the best he'd ever had, but there was so much more to it than that.

So much more.

Her kiss, her taste, the way she looked at him, and the needy way she responded to his touch did something to him and made him feel things he never had before.

Despite wanting to take things slow, the sex had been wild, frantic, and out of control. And while they both might be temporarily sated, he knew he was far from done with her.

He wanted her. Had for a long time now. And he damned well planned to have her again. But he didn't just want her in the bedroom. He wanted to know everything about the woman she was now.

He shifted restlessly and absentmindedly moved his

eggs around on his plate. While he considered this unexpected turn of events, he watched Julia spoon a big chunk
of grapefruit into her mouth. God, that mouth. She looked
warm, content, and completely relaxed, a far cry from how
she'd appeared when she first arrived. If one morning of
lovemaking did this to her, he could only imagine how she'd
feel by the end of the week.

I've waited too long for this, wanted you for too long.

Were they just words spoken in the heat of the moment,
or were they true? She'd never shown any sign of liking him
when they were teens. Hell, she'd even told him he wasn't
her type. A laugh lodged in his throat. Guess she'd changed
her mind on that. But still, he was sure she thought this entire setup was just about sex, and she was in it for a fantasy—
he'd felt the shift in her when she'd come into the barn, knew
that she was trying to act more like her sister. Except deep
down it wasn't an act. There were two sides to this girl, and
he wanted her to understand that when he was buried eight
inches inside her, he knew it was her, *Julia Blair*, and no one
else.

"Coop," Julia said, her laugh breathy, intimate.

"Yeah."

"You're staring at me."

He grinned. "And that makes you uncomfortable?"

"I don't know." She shrugged and fiddled with her
spoon. "Maybe. I guess. I'm not used to guys staring at me
like that."

Then those guys were assholes. The whole lot of them.
Then again, if he caught anyone staring at her like he was,
he'd have no choice but to beat the living shit out of them.

"Like what?" he asked.

She lowered her voice and leaned into him. "Like you want to eat me alive."

Heat prowled through him, and all he could think about was doing just that—kissing her from head to toe before he drove his cock deep inside her.

"Oh, but I do, sweetheart. I do."

Color blossomed high on her cheeks, but that sexy hue reminded him of her pink pussy and how she spread her legs while offering herself up so nicely to him. She wet her lips, and he felt his cock grow another inch.

Fuck.

Coop shifted in his seat. "I told you not to lick your lips like that."

Innocent eyes widened. "Then you should stop saying things like you just did."

"No."

"Oh, and why not?"

"Because I like how you respond."

Memories of the way her body moved under his warmed his blood. Oh, yeah, there really were two sides of her. She bit down on her bottom lip and went quiet. Was she reliving the morning, remembering how well they fit together?

Coop drained the rest of his cup and pushed his plate away. "Are you ready?"

Julia swallowed. "Ready?"

He grinned. "To tackle your chores."

Apprehension passed over her face. "I don't know how—"

"Don't worry." He laughed and added, "I'm not going to make you ride a wild stallion or do anything dangerous."

Her gaze leisurely trailed over him, then taking him by

surprise, she answered with, "Well, I'm pretty sure that stallion already rode me, and maybe I like a little danger."

Jesus.

Talk about poking a bull with a stick. Coop jumped to his feet and almost knocked his chair backward. He grabbed her hand and practically dragged her from the restaurant, all the while ignoring the inquisitive glances aimed their way.

If the guests weren't up and about, he'd have hauled her straight back to the hayloft for round number two. Instead, as soon as he got her alone behind the barn, he pinned her against the wall and kissed her hard. When he finally pulled back, they were breathless.

"You're going to pay for that," he warned.

She feigned innocence. "Pay for what?"

Coop grinned, loving this easy, playful side of her. "Christ, what the hell am I going to do with you?" Before he could tell her exactly what he'd like to do, he spotted Mac and Jess heading into the trails. Mac had his climbing gear with him. The two complemented each other well. While Mac could use some of Jess's calm nature, she could benefit from his wild ways. He couldn't wait to see how their week played out, and hoped like hell in the end Mac won over the girl of his dreams.

He turned his attention back to Julia and inched away. With guests milling about, this was neither the time nor the place to do what he wanted to her.

Looking edgy and breathless, and maybe even a little disappointed that he'd pulled away, Julia gestured with a nod. "Where are they going?"

"We offer rock climbing here." He looked off into the distance. "Just over there, at the base of that mountain."

She planted her hands on her hips. "So, how come those two are off to do fun things, and you're putting me to work?"

"The guys and I all take turns." He grabbed her hand and gave a little tug, leading her inside the barn. "Tomorrow is my day off, and I'll take you up the mountain if you want to go."

"Nope."

Coop laughed and angled his head to see her. "No?"

She pulled a worried face. "I'm not all that coordinated," she admitted, sheepishly taking in the row of horses on her right. "But I would love to go for a ride."

"Have you ever ridden?"

She nodded eagerly, and longing filled her voice when she said, "Yeah, when I was younger." She continued to tell him about the lessons she had in junior high, before he'd met and become best friends with Mari, as Coop gathered the saddles and reins to prepare them for polishing. "I loved it so much." A small smile curled her mouth as she went quiet, like she was remembering something from the past. "Mari and I liked a lot of the same things, but horses were my thing, my passion."

"She wouldn't have been caught dead on one," Coop said.

"I know. I saved all my babysitting money, thinking I could buy my own horse one day. But...well...I stopped riding."

"Why would you stop if you loved it so much?"

"It was expensive, and Mari was just getting into modeling. With the possibility of her making a career out of it, Mom and Dad thought her lessons were a better investment. And obviously they were—look at her now." She gave an easy shrug. "It wasn't like I was ever going to go anywhere with my horseback riding, anyway."

His heart squeezed. "I'm sorry."

Surprise lit her face. "What? No." She gave a quick shake of her head, her long dark hair falling over her shoulders in wild waves, her actions saying so much about her. Julia was kind, caring, always putting the needs of others first, and was probably even happy to sit on the sidelines while her sister stole the show. "It's okay. Really." She clapped her hands and turned her head from left to right. "So where do we start?"

"Right here." Coop leaned in and gave her a tender kiss, determined to put all her needs first and give her the best damn week of her life. She deserved it. In fact, she deserved so much more.

"Oh," she said when he inched back.

Need moved through him at her reaction. He loved that little surprised look, not to mention the heat in her eyes. Christ, as much as he'd love to spend the next few hours losing himself in her, he had chores to do.

He cleared his throat. "Next up is tending to the horses and figuring out which one you want to take out tomorrow."

Before long, they were knee-deep in their chores. They talked quietly about nothing and everything, and while Coop told her all there was to know about the ranch, there was one very private subject he wasn't quite ready to broach— the real reason he was in Alberta. His mother. He'd bought this place for her, and built her a cozy cottage because she'd grown up on a ranch—Coop had lived on one with his folks until middle school, until his father took a job at a bank and they moved across country. Being in familiar surroundings helped with the confusion of her Alzheimer's, but opening up about it to anyone and knowing the inevitable outcome was just too painful to talk about.

His thoughts returned to Julia. He'd watched her throughout the day and couldn't believe how much pleasure she took in feeding, watering, and caring for the horses. It was a damn shame she never had her own. She was a giving person, and he liked that she wasn't afraid of hard work and had readily helped him clean the stalls when he said she could sit that chore out. A few times, he caught her humming to herself. Perhaps, like him, ranch work took her away from her worries and from real life for a few hours.

By the time they finished their chores, breaking only for a late lunch, night was approaching, and they found themselves hot, tired, and hungry. As Coop watched Julia put the mare back in her stall, his hunger turned carnal.

"I like this one," Julia called out after she secured the door behind her.

"And I like this one," Coop said, sneaking up behind her so he could plant a kiss on her neck. But when she spun around, she tripped on a shovel, landing on the hard floor with a *thud*.

"Jesus, Julia, I'm sorry," he hurried out. "I didn't mean to startle you." Looking thoroughly embarrassed, she made a move to get up, but winced when she put weight on her ankle.

Coop scooped her up and set her on a chair. Then he dropped to his knees and took her ankle in his hand.

She tried to squirm away. "It's okay, really."

He felt along her bone. Once he was certain she didn't have a fracture, he said, "Nothing feels broken."

"Thank God, otherwise you might have to put me

down," she joked.

"You're not a horse," he said, grinning. "I think you're going to be okay, but if you want to go into town for an X-ray—"

"No, I'll trust the cowboy to know when a bone is broken or not."

"I think it's just bruised."

"Yeah, that and my ego," she said under her breath.

When he spotted the humiliated look on her face, Coop put his thumb under her chin, an unfamiliar fullness in his chest. "Hey, no need to be embarrassed around me. Besides, this was my fault. I feel terrible that something I did caused you pain." He helped her to her feet, and as he held her against him, she seemed a little breathless, a little shaky.

When their gazes met, his heart hammered, and his entire body reacted as if he'd just been sucker punched. Even with her hair mussed and full of hay, she was breathtaking. Absolutely fucking gorgeous.

He picked hay from her hair. "How about a shower?"

She crinkled her nose. "Good idea." She glanced past his shoulders. "I guess I'd better make my way back to my room."

"No," Coop said, caging her against him. "I don't think you should."

A bit flustered, she said, "I told you my ankle is fine."

"And I told you I don't think you should go to your room."

She lifted one brow. "No? Then how am I supposed to shower?" She looked around. "Unless you have some shower here that I'm not aware—"

"In my room. With me."

Her cheeks turned a pretty shade of pink. For a brief second, he thought he spotted a moment of hesitation, but then she quickly blinked it away, her bravado back in place.

"I'd like that."

He scooped her up and less than five minutes later, he was carrying her into his room on the top floor at the back end of the old farmhouse.

He set her down. "So this is how Chase Cooper lives."

"Sometimes," he said, and circled his hand around her waist. Home was in Nova Scotia, where he had a successful sports medicine practice. But he didn't want to talk about that right now, because that conversation would lead to his mother and the reason he came here often. "Can you walk?"

She rotated her ankle. "It's already feeling better."

"You sure?"

"Positive."

With his fingers on the small of her back, he led her to the bathroom. Desperate to get her naked again, he pulled the shower nozzle, adjusted the temperature to hot, and then turned his attention to her.

Not wanting to waste a moment, his hand went to her T-shirt. He gripped the hem and peeled it from her body. When he exposed her lace bra, air hissed from him, and his heart pounded harder.

"Jesus, I can't tell you how happy I am that you agreed to join me."

She dipped her head to take in the way his hard-on was pressing against his jeans, and in a sexy, teasing voice laced with promise, she responded with, "You don't have to tell me."

Stepping into him, she pushed against his erection,

letting him know in no uncertain terms what she wanted. This time there was no hesitation in her tone, no doubt in her eyes, and he knew with every fiber of his being that here on the ranch, here with him, she was setting another facet of her personality free.

Beneath the reserved package she presented to the world, she was fun, flirtatious, sexy as hell, and damned if he didn't want her to understand that, to embrace that side of herself.

Her hand went to her bra, and she unhooked it from the back. It fell to the floor and exposed her full, gorgeous breasts. Her pale buds hardened beneath his lusty gaze, and he was pretty damn certain he was the luckiest fucking guy on earth.

He stepped back and made quick work of his clothes. He kicked the pile away from his feet, entered the shower stall, and pulled her in with him.

She gasped and laughed as water soaked her clothes. "I'm still dressed."

"I can rectify that." He unzipped her shorts and peeled them down her long legs, and then he gripped her panties to drag them away.

Her breathing changed, became a little faster, and once she was naked, Coop pulled her into the warm stream and held her tight, enjoying the softness of her skin against his. As the hot water fell over them, Julia made a sexy little noise that prompted him into action.

He grabbed the soap and lathered her body, running it over her curves, around her breasts, and between her legs, taking extra care with her sore ankle. Quivering beneath his touch, she moaned with pleasure, and Coop grinned, loving how responsive she was to his touch. Once she was clean, she took the soap and turned it on him. She ran the bar over his body, paying extra attention to his cock. She ran her hands along the length, and the sweet torture made him throb.

"I was thinking," she murmured, and wet her lips.

"About what?" he managed to get out as pleasure forked through him.

She stepped closer, her hands never leaving his cock as she rubbed her hard nipples against his chest. "This time, I want to make you scream for me."

A groan caught in his throat. Truthfully, he loved that she cared about his pleasure, and that she wasn't simply out to take what she could from the cowboy, the way things normally went down on the ranch. But Julia wasn't like those other women, and Coop wasn't a man to take without giving first.

And oh how he planned to give…

He gripped her shoulders, and in a move that seemed to surprise and excite her, he turned her around and braced her hands on the wall. Then he put his mouth close to her ear and said, "Don't move." He heard her breath catch as he slid his hands around her waist to cup both her breasts. "Because in my world, sweetheart, the woman screams first."

As he played with her nipples, he pressed his engorged cock against the small of her back, desperately needing to apply a bit of pressure to help ease the tension. He slipped one hand between her legs until he found her clit. Christ, he loved that she was all wet, swollen, and ready to play.

He stroked her, and she went wild in his arms. Wanton and wicked, she wiggled her ass against his erection, and he nearly abandoned his plan to please her first.

Instead, he slapped her soft, round backside and said, "Stop it."

But naughty little filly that she was, she didn't. She gyrated against him, and the moans in her throat thickened his cock almost painfully.

"You're asking for it," he said. "Keep it up, and I'm going to lose it, and I promised you that I'd take it slow this time."

"Maybe I don't want it slow," she murmured over her shoulder.

Her words, and the desperation behind them, told him so much—she was as needy as he was. Foreign emotions pressed against his heart, knowing she wanted him as badly as he wanted her. She glanced over her shoulder to see him, and when their gazes met, a new intimacy rose between them, one that went deeper than anything he'd ever felt before.

"Julia…" he whispered, and when he caught the emotions in her eyes, he carefully spun her around to face him.

Her fingers tightened on his shoulders, and his flesh burned wherever she touched. "I want you to lose it, Coop," she murmured, impatience lacing her voice as her body began to visibly quake. "Right here in the shower." She went up on her tiptoes and brushed her sex over his erection. "Please."

Sweet Jesus.

Hungering to claim every inch of her, his mind began spinning, but he knew he wanted so much more than just her body. He reached outside the shower, grabbed a condom from the vanity, and quickly sheathed himself. Then he slipped his hands around Julia's ass and lifted her off the floor. He pulled her high onto his waist and slowly began to lower her onto his cock.

"Oh, God, yes," she cried out when he breached her tight opening.

He adjusted his grip and pulled her down hard, dropping her onto his throbbing cock and driving in so deep, she began to claw at his flesh.

He took two measured steps across the tile floor. As he slammed her back against the shower stall, some small, coherent part of his brain warned he was hurting her. "Julia," he said as he struggled for some semblance of control.

She wrapped her legs tighter around his waist.

"Please, Coop. I want you to take me the way you need to."

Fuck. His chest tightened with the way she trusted, the way she gave herself over to him. Air left his lungs in a whoosh. He forgot how to breathe. Warmth streaked through him as he stared at her, taking in the deep-seated need in her eyes. When he began to grow light-headed, he opened his mouth and sucked in a sharp breath.

Her eyes glimmered with dark sensuality, and the unbridled want in her voice when she said, "Fuck me hard, Coop," fragmented his thoughts.

His cock throbbed. There was no fighting back the raging lust weaving its way through his bloodstream. With her back nailed to the wall, he began pounding into her like a junkie in need of a fix.

He'd never *needed* quite like this before.

As he slid deeper and deeper into her slick core, he sank into her warm, wet mouth, savoring the taste of her on his tongue. She began moving urgently over his body, seeking, yearning, demanding more.

While he might be a selfish bastard going at her like some wild, rutting animal, he wasn't about to release until she climaxed for him first. But damned if he wasn't having a hell of a time hanging on.

With her body crushed to his and his cock buried inside her, Julia ran her fingers through his wet hair. "Coop," she cried out. "It's good. So good. Never this good…"

"Same," he groaned, but lost all track of thought when she rotated her hips, sinuously brushing her pelvis over his. She cried out his name, and a moment later, he felt a shudder move through her. Her response drove him to the brink.

"Oh fuck, Julia," he growled and shifted his stance for harder thrusts. He pushed deeper, and when she tightened around his cock, he let go.

He stayed inside her and held her tight. He couldn't bring himself to let her go, was unwilling to break the connection happening between them. But when the water turned cold, he shut off the nozzle, wrapped her in a towel, and carried her to his bed. He pulled back the covers and climbed in with her.

The sex had left him shaken to his core. His heart swelled as he fell deeper in love.

Deeper in love?

Holy Hell, he loved her! He rolled onto his side and drew her close, needing her in his arms, his bed, his life.

"I didn't hurt you, did I?"

Her smile was soft, and when he touched her flesh, trailing his hand over her arm, it occurred to him how warm and welcoming she was. How she felt like forever. Her hand moved to his chest, and he found solace in the heat of her fingers.

"Maybe a little."

She was so sweet. He swallowed and put his hand between her legs, lightly brushing his finger over her, soothing her sex. "Baby, I never meant to hurt you."

"But it's a good hurt."

Tenderness rushed through him. "Hurt is hurt." He covered her with a sheet, slid off the bed, and hurried to the bathroom. He grabbed a washcloth and ran it under the warm water.

"This will help." Her eyes dropped from his to the cloth as he sat beside her on the bed and drew down the sheet. "Open for me."

She spread her legs, and he placed the warm cloth on her sex. Her eyes widened and her mouth formed a little O.

"Feel better?" he asked.

She nodded as he tended to her, desperate to take care of the girl he'd fallen for all over again and intended to keep forever.

Chapter Seven

Julia stretched out on her bed and glanced at the gorgeous man asleep beside her. Here it was, five glorious days since the plane had first deposited her on the ranch, and she couldn't deny that she was having the best time of her life. They'd spent their days riding the trails, picnicking, hanging out with his friends at the saloon, and making love in the sun—not to mention all the naughty things they did in his private pond—and she didn't even mind the day they spent doing chores. In fact, she quite enjoyed it. Working with her hands allowed her to shelve her worries and forget about real life for a while—and that this fantasy would soon come to an end.

The truth was, she'd decided to gift herself with a week of relaxation and had no desire to think about real life. Nope, she wasn't going to delve into his personal life at all. Not that he wanted to share that side of himself anyway. This was about casual sex and nothing else, and she was determined to spend her time enjoying life on the ranch and all the sex Coop had to offer. No questions asked.

By God, the man got to her in so many ways. But it was temporary.

It wasn't like a relationship could work. Not only was he into wild, carefree women, but he lived here, and she lived halfway across the country.

Julia gave a hard shake of her head and berated herself for dreaming about something more permanent. For one, it was her sister Coop had invited to the ranch, and two, she was pretending to be something she wasn't. But she couldn't deny that she enjoyed playing the part of a wild and wicked woman. How would she ever go back to dull and drab Julia?

Warm morning sun fell over the bed as Coop rolled onto his side, pulling the blankets with him. She smiled, and since they'd made love well into the wee hours of the morning, she decided to let him sleep while she went to the pond for an early-morning swim.

She made a move to climb from the bed, but his arm darted out to stop her.

"Going somewhere?" he asked.

Taking in his rumpled, sleepy state, which made him look so damn sexy, Julia laughed and fell back onto the bed with him. "I was going to take a swim because I thought you were asleep."

"You thought wrong." His smile was devilish, full of mischief. "Now come here."

He pulled her on top of him, and they exchanged a long, heated look before he gave her a kiss full of passion. As he took her mouth, he stole her breath, and her heart missed a beat. She'd just lectured herself on keeping this sexual, but when he kissed her like that, she had no idea how she was ever going to walk away when this was over. He inched back, and when she met his glance, the warmth in his gaze and the ache of desire in the depth of his eyes filled her with longing. She craved so much more from him.

Despite a long night of lovemaking, she wanted him again. As if he could read her thoughts, he grabbed a condom from the night table and rolled it on.

Not wanting to think about what this man was doing to her, or how hard she'd fallen for him, she sat up and straddled him, conveying without words what she wanted. With a sexy grin on his face, Coop touched her leg. Heat rippled over her sex when he began a lazy journey up her thigh. When he reached her hips, he lifted her up off him, and then settled her back down on his hard cock.

She took in a breath, and her whole body trembled as she let it out. The pleasure was intense, glorious, and so deeply intimate she found it difficult to keep her emotions in check. "Coop," she cried out as he filled her, quivering as his cock reached deep.

He brushed his thumb over her, and turbulent eyes full of heat met hers. "I know, Julia. Believe me, I know."

With that, they began moving together, their hands touching each other all over, like neither could get enough. His muscles rippled as pressure built inside her, and there was more going on here than just sex. At least for her.

He was everything she wanted, everything she craved. She pinched her eyes shut and berated herself, because this was supposed to be just about sex, and when she stopped pretending, Coop would be bored with the real Julia.

"Julia," Coop murmured, powering his hips upward. He

took her slowly, like he was savoring every second. "Look at me."

When she opened her eyes, he slipped his hand around her head and drew her mouth to his. The thumb on his other hand moved between her legs, brushing over her clit as he kissed her softly and with such passion she began burning from the inside out.

As her body began trembling, Coop used slow, easy thrusts, pushing her higher and higher while he dragged his thumb over her sensitive bundle of nerves. Unlike their frantic lovemaking sessions, this was sensual, unhurried, and tender, but every bit as potent.

Her muscles clenched, and she was free-falling without a net. As she tumbled into climax, they both cried out in ecstasy, falling over the precipice at the same time.

A long time later, when she finally came back down to earth, she collapsed on top of him, and he circled his hands around her waist to hold her tight. She listened to his heartbeat, and as it pounded in his chest, she wondered how she'd ever be able go back to the way things were before this incredible week.

When her legs started to grow numb, she rolled off him, and he packaged her against his body. She savored every minute while she still could. A soft, contented noise sounded in his throat, and when she glanced up, Coop gave her a lethargic smile and lazily ran his thumb up and down her arm.

"You're kind of rocking my world," he murmured, before dropping a gentle kiss onto her forehead.

In need of a distraction—before she did something crazy like tell him how she felt—she began tracing the outline of his face.

He gave a rough moan of pleasure. "Christ, if you keep touching me like that, I'm going to pin you down and take you again, and I know you're too sore for that."

"Oh," she said as a thrill moved through her. She loved how she affected him—how he affected her—but in two short days, when the plane came to collect her, she'd never see him again.

She ran her finger over his crooked nose, and even though this week was supposed to be about casual sex—not about her getting to know him on a deeper level—curiosity finally got the better of her and she asked, "How did you break your nose?"

But as soon as the words left her mouth, everything between them changed. Coop went silent and cast his eyes down in deep thought. As his bliss disappeared, his body tensed, and he gripped her hand to still her exploration. He angled his head toward the window, away from her view, and once again she couldn't help but wonder about his secrets.

He didn't answer her, and while the lawyer in her was used to getting answers, and she was never passive in the courtroom, she was a bit hesitant to pry with him. Getting personal wasn't in her best interest.

"I know this week was about sex, and just having fun, so I get that you don't want to delve into your personal business." She shrugged, trying to make light of things, despite the rawness in her throat. She stole a quick glance at the clock and continued to ramble on. "Soon enough I'll be heading back to the real world and leaving this fantasy behind." She gave him a smile and plucked at the bedding, like she did this sort of thing all the time. "It was good while it lasted, though, wasn't it?"

• • •

It was good while it lasted?

He swallowed against the tightness in his throat. How could she still not see what she meant to him? Her plane left in two days, and if he couldn't convince her that it was *her* he'd wanted all along, he was damn well going to lose her. No fucking way would he let that happen. She was the one and only girl for him, and he damn well planned to fight for her until her eyes were wide open and she saw this for what it was. Love. He grabbed a fistful of hair and tugged, blood pounding through his veins. He needed to do something, and he needed to do it now. Never had he felt like he had more on the line.

"Coop?" she said. "Are you okay?"

"Yeah, come on." He jumped from the bed and pulled her up with him. If he wanted her to trust him, to see that he wanted more than just sex, then he'd have to give more in return. That meant letting her get a glimpse into his life and opening up about his mother, no matter how painful it was to talk about it. He probably should have told her a long time ago he was a sports doctor, and that he usually only traveled to the ranch on weekends, but kept his mouth shut knowing it would lead to questions he wasn't ready to answer. But it was that silence that was standing in the way of her seeing his real intentions. An uneasy feeling tightened his gut. When he opened up, would she be angry that he kept so much from her? Would she leave and never look back? Shit.

"Where are we going?" she asked.

This week had been about her, but now maybe it was time to be about him. "For a ride." After a shower, they dressed and made their way outside. She kept casting curious glances his way, but he remained tight-lipped. Twenty minutes later they were in one of the ranch's pickup trucks.

He felt her eyes on him and turned to see her looking at him with curiosity. "What are you up to?"

"What?" he said, laughing. A pickup truck came his way, and he waved to the driver as it passed. "I just thought we'd go get a beaver tail."

"A beaver tail?"

"You do know what a beaver tail is, don't you?" he teased.

"Of course I do. I *am* Canadian."

"I've been craving a peanut butter and banana tail." He cast her another glance as he drove along the back road to town. "You like them, right?"

"Fried pastry topped with all sorts of candy. What's not to like? I guess I just never thought of you as a beaver tail kind of guy."

"Not manly?" he questioned, giving her a half-cocked smile.

"How could it *not* be manly?" She laughed. "Every big strong guy I know eats peanut butter and banana pastry."

"You think I'm big and strong."

"Oh, my, God," she said, laughing as she rolled her eyes.

He grinned. "What's your favorite?"

"I'm kind of partial to the cinnamon and sugar." She looked out her window. "I can't believe there is a actually a franchise out here in the middle of nowhere."

"There's a town nearby, lots of shops and stores."

"Oh?" Her eyes lit, and she probed, "Do you go often?"

"Not anymore. I don't really have time, but I spent a lot of time there as a kid."

Her brow crinkled. "You did?"

He waved a hand toward the pastures as they drove past. "I grew up around here."

Her head jerked back. "You did? When did you move east?"

"Middle school."

"I guess I just thought you'd always lived there."

"Nope." He drove a few more miles and then pulled off the road. He rolled the windows down, and a warm breeze scented with horses and hay drifted through the cab of the truck. "See that house?" he said, pointing to an old ranch in the distance. She nodded and he explained, "That's where I grew up."

She sat up, intrigued, and stuck her head out the window. "Really?"

"Yep." He pointed to the corner room. "That was my bedroom. And you see that tree house?" He pointed to the big old maple at the side of the house.

"Yeah."

"Dad and I built that." At the mention of his dad he felt a little melancholy. He missed him so much. He gazed at Julia and smiled. His dad would have loved her. He'd have spent hours telling her about his childhood antics, and she would have laughed, loving every minute of it.

She pulled her head back in. "I remember your dad. He was always very nice when I went into the bank." She looked a bit hesitant. "Is he…"

"No, he's gone now," he explained.

"I'm sorry."

He reached out and squeezed her hand, taking comfort in her touch. "It's okay. Are your folks still alive?"

"Yes. Dad retired from the service and is now puttering around the house fixing things."

A truck sped by, kicking up dust. Coop rolled the windows up to protect her hair and clothes from getting soiled. "Fixing things?"

She laughed. "Okay, more like getting on Mom's nerves. He needs a hobby."

Coop laughed with her. "When I retire, I'm getting a motorcycle." He held his hands out and rolled them, mimicking the action of riding.

"How about your mom, Coop?"

"She's...okay," he said and pulled back onto the highway. He could tell she wanted to ask more, and while he planned to tell her—to share everything with her—he wanted to do it later.

He drove toward town, and she squeezed his hand. "I liked seeing your childhood home."

"Good, because I have more to show you."

"Oh?" she said, her eyes moving over his body. "What exactly do you have in mind?"

He laughed at her playful side. "Hey, get your mind out of the gutter."

She chuckled along with him, and they fell into easy conversation as he drove the rest of the way. A short while later he pulled into a parking spot along the town's main street.

He shaded his eyes and glanced up and down the long street. "Nothing much has changed in twenty years. Except maybe the new beaver tail and ice cream store."

She turned, taking it all in. "It's so quaint. I love it."

His heart warmed. It meant something to him that she liked where he'd grown up. "Yeah?"

"Yeah. I can see why you'd want to move back here."

He captured her hand and pulled her to him as he led her down the sidewalk and into the store. They both ordered a pastry, and he guided her to the playground he hung out at when he was young. Kids bustled about around them, their parents talking on park benches as they played.

"Swing?" he asked.

"Sure."

They grabbed the empty swings beside each other and dived into their pastries.

"This is where you hung out?" she asked.

He wiped cinnamon from her face, and when she gave him a sheepish look, his heart turned over. She was so sweet, and he was so fucking lucky to have her in his life. Now, just to keep her there. "This swing exactly," he said.

"Cool." The smile she gave him warmed his soul. He bit into his pastry, catching a big hunk of banana, and moaned with pleasure.

"It's so good, isn't it?" She took another big bite, chewed, and said, "I can't remember the last time I had one."

"You should have one every day," he said.

"Yeah." She scoffed. "Wouldn't my hips love that?"

A hyper little girl in pigtails squealed and started to run by, then slowed when she saw their food. Her eyes went wide. "Mom," she shrieked. "I want a beaver tail."

Julia crinkled her nose. "Uh-oh. Look what we started."

More kids started yelling, and he cringed. "I think the last thing any of them need is sugar."

"You don't like kids," she said, a statement, not a question.

"Yes, I do."

Her head came up with a start, surprise in her eyes. "Really?"

He dragged his feet though the dirt as he moved on the swing. "Yeah. Someday I'd like to have a couple."

"Oh."

"Oh what?"

"Nothing…I just…nothing."

He kicked his leg out, to pick up momentum as he swung beside her. "I'll teach them how to play soccer, hockey…ride a horse."

She smiled at him. "I bet you'd be a great dad."

"What about you? You want kids?"

"I haven't given it too much thought. The last few years have been spent focusing on my career."

"But you do want them?"

"Yeah, I do."

"Good."

She gave him a strange look as they finished their last bites. Coop jumped off the swing, grabbed her hand, and hauled her to him.

"I thought we'd go for a spin." He pointed to the merry-go-round. "I swear I could get that thing going a hundred miles an hour. I'll teach my kids that, too."

"I think I'm going to pass."

"Seriously?"

She put her hand on her stomach. "Unless you want a second viewing of my dessert."

He laughed, and she looked so adorable as she grinned

up at him that he couldn't help himself. He leaned in and put his lips on hers, tasting the sweet cinnamon on her tongue.

"You taste good," he murmured. "I think they should only ever make peanut butter, banana, and cinnamon-flavored beaver tails."

"Maybe I can get a law passed," she teased. She broke the kiss and grabbed his hand, a new excitement in her eyes. "Show me where else you hung out."

"Sure." He loved her enthusiasm and how interested she was in knowing more about him.

He led her along the streets, taking her to the park where he and his friends skateboarded, past the school where he went to elementary, along a side street where some of his childhood friends had grown up, then stopped at the old movie house.

When he saw that it was some chick flick playing, he said, "You're not going to make me, are you?"

She sagged against him and gave him a playful grin. "You bet I am."

"Fine, then, but we're sitting in the back so we can make out."

"Oh, is that what you used to do when you were a kid?"

"No, but only because I was too young."

She gave him a playful whack, and he reached for his wallet. He bought their tickets and found seats at the back of the near-empty theater. The movie came on, and true to his word, he spent the better part of the time kissing her. From the way she kissed him back, she didn't seem to mind missing the flick. By the time the credits rolled, it was well past dinnertime, and they walked back to his truck.

"Dinner at the saloon?" he asked.

Her cheeks were flushed from their heavy make-out session. "I'm thinking more along the lines of dinner in bed."

He hurried his steps and dragged her along with him. "You don't have to ask me twice."

He opened her door for her, stepped back, and waited for her to get in. Instead, she stopped, turned to him, and put her hand on his chest. His throat tightened. Had she changed her mind? Was she pushing him away? His stomach dropped, but then she reached up and laid her hand on his cheek. A surge of warmth flooded his veins at the softness of her palm on his jaw, the rasp of his stubble against the pad of her thumb as it slid gently over his face. Such a small thing, this show of affection, so genuine that for a moment he held his breath, fearful that even pulling air into his lungs would break the incredible connection between them. She looked up at him, and the tenderness in her eyes became his undoing. His knees buckled, and he forced them straight as he leaned into her hand, overwhelmed with the things she made him feel.

"I really liked seeing where you grew up," she said softly, and then she smiled. The faintest lift of the corner of her mouth. "Thanks for sharing it with me." Her hand slipped from his cheek, and the loss of her touch left an emptiness in his chest. He stood there trying to remember how to breathe as she slid into the truck.

She was quiet on the way home, her glance straying to his numerous times as he drove. Whenever he returned it, she gave him a warm smile. They reached the ranch, and he circled the truck to open her door. She jumped out, and he was about to guide her inside when she went up on her tiptoes and planted a soft kiss on his mouth. He slid his hand around her waist and drew her in close, needing the connection. As he held her, his body reacted with need.

"It seems like you might have a little something else to show me," she teased as his erection pressed against her stomach.

"It does seem that way," he said, and brushed his thumb over her cheek, wanting her so much he felt dizzy. "And there's nothing little about it."

She laughed and swatted him again, making him feel like the teenage boy who was so crazy about her.

In seconds flat he had her naked and on the bed. He kissed her mouth, her neck, her breasts, basking in her sweetness. Unable to wait another second, he sheathed himself and pushed into her. Her hand touched his back, and he sucked in a breath as heat zinged through him. Christ, he was lost. So fucking lost in her.

His mouth moved back to hers, and she slid her tongue over his bottom lip. He drew it into his mouth, so aware of how well their bodies fit together. Blood pounded through his veins, and her nipples pressed against his chest as they rocked into each other, need propelling them on. Her muscles clenched around him, her whole body trembling beneath his.

"Yes," she murmured, and the second he felt her warm heat, he let go.

"Julia, baby," he murmured into her mouth. He put his hands on either side of her head and inched up to see her face. She stared at him for an endless moment, then her fingers tangled through his hair. She gave a throaty purr of contentment, and his heart filled with so much love. His brain raced. He could take her every night like this, yet never get enough of her.

He rolled off her, discarded the condom, and then covered her with a warm blanket. She sank into him, and they
remained quiet for a long time, both lost in their thoughts.
When he could finally breathe again, he rolled on his side.
His heart turned inside out to see her so sated, so comfortable with him that she'd already started to drift off to sleep.

"Julia."

He touched her face, pulling her awake. Her eyes met
his, and the smile she gave him tugged at the center of his
chest. He needed to tell her everything, and pray to God
that she didn't think he'd been keeping himself emotionally
closed off because all he ever wanted was sex from her.

"Yeah?" she asked.

"We need to talk."

Chapter Eight

Julia's stomach turned upside down. She'd thought something significant had happened between them today. Thought Coop had opened up to her, showing her another side of himself, because he might want more. But now he needed to talk, and in her book, that meant one thing. It was over. God, how could she have been such a fool to think, even for the briefest of moments, that things could have ended differently? Then again, even if he had wanted more, she'd been playing a part, which meant he didn't know the *real* her. If he'd fallen for anyone—again—it was her sister.

She braced herself. "What is it?"

He opened his mouth, but his cell phone rang. He leaped from the bed and grabbed it. What—or who—was so important that it couldn't wait a minute?

Julia listened to the one-sided conversation, barely able to comprehend what was going on. When he finished talking, he shut down his phone and said, "I have to go."

Before she could even ask what was going on, he disappeared into the bathroom. When he came out, he dressed quickly.

He turned to her, worry backlighting his eyes as he said, "We'll talk later."

She nodded, and he practically ran out the door. Stunned by his sudden departure, Julia climbed from the bed and numbly made her way to the shower. He was about to break it off with her. Should she just leave, get a lift into town until the next plane came?

After washing, she pulled on a dress and walked to her window to pull open the sheer curtain. But when she did, she spotted Coop and Tessa talking on the wraparound deck of the small cottage at the foot of the mountain. At least now she knew *who* was so important. Julia had no idea what they were saying, but she could tell by the tension in their posture that they were discussing something very important, something very personal.

Unease moved through her as the sting of jealousy hit her hard. Her heart began racing, aching painfully, but she quickly tried to shrug it off and reminded herself that she had no claims on Coop. They weren't dating, and he was likely only seconds from reminding her this was a week of sex and nothing else.

Feeling slightly light-headed, she backed away from the window. No matter how much her brain tried to convince her that Coop didn't matter, her heart knew he did. Cripes, she never should have gotten on that plane, or engaged in a wild week of sun and sex.

She'd pretended to be the kind of woman he wanted to get him to like her, but deep down she most definitely wasn't the kind of girl who could love casually.

Needing to get far away from the place, she grabbed her purse and hurried downstairs, looking for a ranch hand who could drive her to town, or possibly get her a cab. But when she stepped onto the wooden deck, she ran into a big muscular wall—Coop.

He gripped her shoulders to still her. "Julia—" he began, then looked down at the way she was clutching her purse. Worried, he did a careful assessment of her face. Her stomach lurched. How would she ever go on without him? "Are you going somewhere?" he asked.

"I'm leaving. I'm going to stay in town until the plane comes."

Visibly taken aback, his hands tightened on her shoulders, and his body stiffened. "What the hell?"

"It's okay, Coop."

"Like fuck it's okay," he bit out, his face tightening warily. "What, you were just going to leave, without telling me?"

"I have to go." She tried to push away, but he wouldn't let her go. "Coop—"

"You're not making sense," he cut in, a strain in his voice she'd never heard before. "After today…I thought…"

"You don't owe me any explanation." In the distance she caught a glimpse of Tessa. "What you do in your private life is none of my business. I knew what I was getting myself into when I decided to stay here." Okay, she was rambling, but she couldn't seem to help herself. What the hell happened to the calm, collected lawyer who always thought with her head and not her heart?

Coop got quiet for a moment, and then a muscle in his jaw rippled. "Did you, Julia? Did you really know what you were getting yourself into?"

"What? Yes, of course."

Coop stared at her longer than was comfortable, then grabbed her hand and tugged. "Come with me."

Her stomach tightened as he marched her toward the cottage, and she had to hurry her steps to keep up. "Coop, I don't think this is a good idea."

"There is someone I want you to meet." The tension in his tone was replaced by sadness. A sadness so deep she felt it in her core. "Someone very important to me," he added with a whisper.

The protest went out of her as he walked her across the field and eased open the door to the cottage. Julia's nervous glance landed on Tessa, who exchanged a knowing look with Coop before disappearing into the other room. After the pretty brunette exited, the sight of the elderly lady sitting at one end of a floral sofa came into view.

"Coop," Julia asked quietly. "What's going on?"

Just then the woman turned her head, and Coop started for her.

"Mom, it's okay. It's me, Coop." He hurried out and ducked in time to dodge the remote control aimed his way. He picked the remote up and set it on the sofa.

Her heart ached as she watched Coop drop to his knees in front of his mother. He took her hand in his and was speaking quietly to her, soothing words for her ears only. Understanding dawned quickly. This was the curveball life had thrown him. Her throat tightened, and her legs weakened beneath her. A few moments later, the woman blinked and turned to face Julia.

"This is Julia," Coop said, standing back up. Warmth

moved into his eyes when they met hers, and she nearly forgot how to breathe, the love she felt for him twisting inside her. "Julia, this is my moth—"

"Are you in Chase's class?"

Julia looked at his mother, then back at Coop in search of answers. When he nodded, she took a tentative step closer.

"Yes, I am."

His mother frowned. "Chase's friends don't come around much anymore, and he's never brought a girl home before."

"That's because this one is special, Mom."

Her smile returned, and with hands gnarled from arthritis, she waved Julia over. "Come let me have a look at you."

Julia took a few measured steps toward the sofa, and as she neared, Coop held his hand out to her. She took the offered hand, and when she slid her palm into his, he gave a reassuring squeeze.

"Julia, I'd like you to meet Lois, my mother."

"It's a pleasure to meet you, Lois."

"She's a very pretty one, Chase. I can see why you like her."

Julia dropped down onto the sofa next to Coop's mother, and when she took Lois's hand in hers, she didn't miss the way Coop's tense shoulders relaxed, or the mixture of pride and possessiveness on his face when his glance met hers.

Julia turned her attention to the television to take note of the soap opera Lois was watching. "I see you're watching *The Rich and the Famous*. It's one of my favorites," Julia said.

That brought a smile to Lois's face. "Mine too, dear."

With her heart full of all the things she felt for Coop, Julia spent a few more minutes talking about the characters, having become familiar with the show when an old friend joined the cast a few years back, but then suddenly, a confused look came over Lois's face and her lids began to flicker.

"I think she needs to rest now," Coop said quietly.

Understanding that Coop needed a moment alone with his mother, Julia stood and gestured toward the door. "I should—"

He gave a quick shake of his head and placed his palm on her face. "Please stay."

She nodded, the heat of his hand stirring all her emotions. Coop was sharing a very private part of his life with her, and if he wanted her there with him, then she was damn well going to be there for him. He put a blanket over his mother, and as he worked to make her comfortable, all of the pieces known as Chase Cooper fell into place. Tears pricked her eyes, because the boy she knew from high school had turned into the most amazing man she'd ever met.

"Julia."

His soft voice startled her, and she blinked the moisture from her eyes.

There was a tenderness in his eyes as they moved over her face. "Are you okay?"

"I didn't know."

"Who's there?" his mother bellowed, and Julia jumped.

"Mom, it's me, Coop." He turned, just as his mother threw the remote at him again, and he caught it in the shoulder. It clattered to the floor, and Tessa rushed in to help his mother as he picked it up.

There was a real sadness on his face, but he tried to inject humor when he pointed to his nose and said, "Sometimes she has great aim."

Her heart squeezed. "I'm so sorry."

"Come with me." He captured her hand, and the two made their way back outside.

Julia glanced around at the wide expanse of land and took Coop's situation into consideration. "You bought the ranch and moved here for your mother."

It was a statement, not a question, but he answered anyway. "Yes and no."

Her glance darted back to his, and all she wanted to do was take him into her arms and hold him, soothe him, tell him everything would be all right. "Yes and no?"

Coop leaned against the white railing and pulled her into him, his legs wrapping around hers. He took a deep breath, let it out slowly, and began, "Yes, I bought it for my mother because she grew up on a ranch, and the familiarity helps with her Alzheimer's. The guys chipped in on it with me because I couldn't afford it by myself. And no, I didn't move here."

Confused, she asked, "What do you mean you didn't move here?"

"I don't live here, Julia. I live in Kentville."

"Kentville?" Okay, that took her by surprise. "As in an hour outside of Halifax?"

"I'm a sports medicine doctor, and I have a practice there that I can't just up and leave."

She widened her eyes. That's how he knew about her ankle. "Why didn't you tell me any of this?" As soon as the question left her mouth, she shook her head, already knowing the answer. "Wait, never mind." She waved a finger back and forth between the two of them. "This situation wasn't about us getting to know each other." She inched back, and she could feel his tension like it was her own when he cupped her elbow and hauled her closer.

"Oh, no you don't. You're not going anywhere, and you've got it all wrong."

"Coop, please," she said, needing to put a measure of distance between them.

Wait. Did he just say I had it all wrong?

"Getting to know each other was my every intention." He glanced down, then back at her. "I just didn't talk about any of this because it's…it's hard. She's very sick…" His voice wavered when he added, "She doesn't have much time."

Her heart twisted at the sadness on his face. "I'm sorry, Coop."

"I wanted to tell you." He brushed his hand over his chin, and the vulnerability she detected in the depth of his eyes had her taking a small, tentative step toward him. "I planned to tell you tonight." He put his hand on her cheek, and she leaned in to it.

"You did."

"Yeah, I didn't want you to think I was holding back because I only wanted sex."

Her hand closed over his. "You…you want more than sex?"

"Don't you see?" he asked, a new urgency in his voice. "I'm crazy about you, Julia. Today I took you to my old hang-outs because I wanted you to get to know me. To show you that I wanted more. What you said in the bedroom, about this being a fantasy. I never once thought this thing between us wasn't real."

If her heart beat any faster it was going to burst from her chest. "Really?"

Coop placed his finger under her chin to tip it up. "I

meant what I said."

"What did you say?"

"When I told my mother you were special, I meant it," he said, his voice thinning to a whisper.

Her knees buckled, and she forced them to straighten. "You did?"

He brushed his thumb over her cheek. "Julia, sweetheart. I need you in my life. It's always been you I wanted."

Her entire body tightened. "Then why did you invite Mari here for the week?"

He put his arm around her, and all she could think about was how good it felt to be held by him.

"Late one night, after a few beers, the guys and I got to talking about the ones that got away."

"Oh." She looked down as she chewed on that. Coop thought Mari was the one who'd gotten away, and since she was pretending to be her, Mari was the girl he'd fallen for again.

"But I was wrong, Julia." He shook his head. "I was so wrong."

Julia swallowed. "Wrong? How?"

"Your sister wasn't the one who got away. Right after I sent that invitation, I started having second thoughts and regretted my spur-of-the-moment decision. She's not the girl for me. She never was."

Confused, she faltered backward, her mind racing, trying to keep up.

"Oh, no you don't," he said again, putting his hand around her waist to bring her back.

"Coop?"

"You're not getting away from me again."

"What are you talking about?"

"You, Julia. You were the one who got away. I'm in love with you. You never paid me a lick of attention all those years ago, but now that I've got you, I'm not letting you go. I don't want anyone but you, Julia. I never have."

He was in love with her? If only that were true.

She shook her head, her stomach clenching as she poked her thumb into her chest. "What you don't understand is it's not me you're falling for. I was living out a fantasy, pretending to be carefree like my sister, so really, it was her you were falling for all over again."

"I never fell for her once, so how can I be falling for her again?"

"What are you talking about?"

"Mari and I were only ever friends. It was you I always liked, but there's an unwritten rule that I had to live by: you don't hit on your best friend's sister. And of course, you did tell me I wasn't your type."

"But I thought you two…"

"You thought wrong. And all this pretending you thought you were doing, well, you weren't pretending at all. You've always just suppressed that side of yourself. "

"Coop—" she began, but he cut her off.

"Maybe pretending to be wild and happy-go-lucky like your sister is what gave you the courage you needed to just let go and be yourself."

Clearly, he was missing the point here. "I wasn't myself. It wasn't really *me* you were having a wild week with, or thought things were real with."

"That's bullshit, Julia," he said, his voice a little lower, a little harsher. "It was you, and I'm not going to let you think otherwise." He grabbed her hand. "Come with me. I'm going to prove it to you that I knew it was *you* who I was with this week." He led her to the barn. "I was saving this surprise for later, but well. I think you need to see it now."

He pulled open one of the stalls that had been empty up until now, and Julia looked in.

"Coop?" she asked when she saw the pretty mare. "What's going on?"

He turned to her and put his arms on her shoulders. "She's yours," he said, his voice rough with emotions.

Her brain stalled. "Mine?"

"She's all yours, babe. Yours to take care of and to ride when you're here, and I want you here, with me, a lot. She just needs a name."

Julia's hands went to her face as her throat tightened. "No, I can't."

"Sure you can."

He gently touched her cheek, and the gesture brought tears to her eyes. "It's too much."

Just then the mare whinnied and poked Julia with her muzzle. Coop laughed. "I think she likes you. Not that I can blame her."

Julia stepped closer and ran her hands over the mare's forehead, examining the horse through blurry eyes. No one had ever given her a gift like this before. "She's beautiful. Everything I've ever wanted." She sniffed and said, "I can't believe you did this."

"I have something else for you."

She looked into his eyes, and the love she saw there filled her with warm longing. He reached into the stall and grabbed something. She shook her head and laughed when she saw the daisy-duke shorts and pink riding crop.

"What are those for?"

"You've been wearing Tessa's clothes all week, and I thought you might want something of your own."

"And you had to find the shortest shorts in the universe?" God, she loved him. She loved him so much, she was ready to explode from the inside out.

He gave her a grin that weakened her knees. "Well…yeah."

She shook her head and took the pink crop. She ran her hand along the length of it, stroking it with her fingers, and Coop groaned as he watched the action. "And this?"

He shrugged. "You've never seen a riding crop before?"

She looked at the mare. "I have, yes, but I could never use this on her."

He took it from her and flicked it against her ass. "Who says it's for the horse?"

The cheek of her ass had received the sting of the crop, but it was the unexpected clench of her sex that brought her breath out with a soft moan. "Oh."

"Don't you see, this is the real you, Julia. I've always known that, and the horse and crop represent both sides." He drew her into his arms, and she slid her hands around his back. He pressed a kiss to her forehead and said, "Beneath the beauty and brains, you're fun-loving, sexy as hell, kind, caring, and so easy to be with. You just suppressed that side of yourself because you're sweet and giving and are always putting everyone else's needs above your own. But I'm not going to let you do that anymore. You have needs, too, and I'm going to see that they're taken care of." He flicked the crop over her backside again and grinned. "Every single one of them."

Julia stood there blinking up at him, trying to absorb everything he was telling her. Coop wanted her. *Her*. Julia Blair.

"Do you believe me now?" he asked. "Believe that I *know* who I was sleeping with this week?"

"I do," she said around the lump in her throat, everything she felt for this man making her head spin and her heart swell.

"Good, because you see, Julia, when I asked you if you knew what you were getting yourself into, you really didn't, because the second you stepped off that plane, I was determined to make you mine. When I said I was glad you were here, I meant it."

"I'm glad I came, too."

"I want *you*, Julia. I always have."

Her pulse pounded in her neck, her heart swelling. "I've always wanted you, too," she admitted.

Grinning, he lightly brushed his thumb over her bottom lip. "So I am your type?"

"Yeah," she said. "I have a thing for those manly types who eat peanut butter and banana beaver tails."

He laughed and scooped her up.

"Where are you taking me?" she asked.

"To the pond, then the loft, and then my bed." As he began ticking off all the places they'd made love, an invisible fist clenched around her heart.

"Don't forget the pasture," she added, her heart soaring.

"Oh, don't worry. I haven't forgotten a single thing." He grinned.

Julia arched a brow. "Oh really? Do tell."

"Actually," he said, a mischievous grin spreading across

his face. "I'm tired of talking."

"Well, I must say," she began, embracing the wild side of herself and feeling free for the first time in her life, "I do love a man of action."

He planted a warm kiss on her mouth and said, "And I love *you*, Julia Blair. The girl who is smart, sexy, wild, and wicked." He stopped to give her a wink before he added, "The girl who loves horses, and riding, and has yet to be punished for that stallion comment."

Never happier, joy welled up inside Julia, and a squeal of delight sounded deep in her throat. Coop squeezed her tighter, and with her body in his arms and her heart in his hands, he led her to the ladder leading to the upstairs loft. Julia smiled up at him, embracing the two sides of herself, and knowing there was no other man she'd trust with both.

Acknowledgments

First and foremost a huge thank you to my amazing editor Candace Havens. Thank you for believing in this series and helping me make the stories shine. You are a rock star! I'm looking forward to working with you on more books.

My husband definitely needs to be mentioned in this acknowledgement. I can always count on him to listen to me ramble, or brainstorm when I'm stuck. Most times I think he's tuned me out, as he mainly sits there staring at me blankly. But then he tosses out brilliant ideas that I usually run with.

Danita, thank you for keeping me organized and sane. You are a true gem, and I value your PA services, and your friendship.

To all the fabulous members of Foxy Fiction. You are all my extended family and the support you give me is phenomenal. Thank you all!

About the Author

New York Times and *USA Today* bestselling author Cathryn Fox is a wife, mom, sister, daughter, and friend. She loves dogs, sunny weather, anything chocolate (she never says no to a brownie) pizza and red wine. Cathryn has two teenagers who keep her busy and a husband who is convinced he can turn her into a mixed martial arts fan. When not writing, Cathryn can be found laughing over lunch with friends, hanging out with her kids, or watching a big action flick with her husband.

Also by Cathryn Fox...

HOLD ME DOWN HARD

When Eden Carver, Iowa farm girl turned NY actress, decides to seduce the sexy cop next door, she begins to wonder if she's bitten off more than she can chew. The last thing Officer Jay Bennett wants is to cross a line with the sweet and innocent country girl. A naïve girl like Eden doesn't belong in his dangerous world. He knows he needs to walk away from temptation, but when sweet little Eden bites back, it tilts his world on its axis. Because biting back changes everything.

Made in United States
Cleveland, OH
08 May 2025

16774075R00069